Island
of Ogres

Island
of Ogres

Lensey Namioka

TUTTLE PUBLISHING
Boston • Rutland, Vermont • Tokyo

This edition first published in 2005 by Tuttle Publishing, an imprint of Periplus Editions (HK) Ltd., with editorial offices at 364 Innovation Drive, North Clarendon, VT 05759

Originally published in 1989 by Harper & Row, Publishers.

Library of Congress Control Number: 2005923975
ISBN 0-8048-3612-4

Distributed by

North America, Latin America & Europe
Tuttle Publishing
364 Innovation Drive
North Clarendon, VT 05759-9436
Tel: (802) 773-8930
Fax: (802) 773-6993
info@tuttlepublishing.com
www.tuttlepublishing.com

Asia Pacific
Berkeley Books Pte. Ltd.
130 Joo Seng Road
#06-01/03 Olivine Building
Singapore 368357
Tel: (65) 6280-1330
Fax: (65) 6280-6290
inquiries@periplus.com.sg
www.periplus.com

Japan
Tuttle Publishing
Yaekari Building, 3rd Floor
5-4-12 Ōsaki
Shinagawa-ku
Tokyo 141 0032
Tel: (03) 5437-0171
Fax: (03) 5437-0755
tuttle-sales@gol.com

First printing
09 08 07 06 05   10 9 8 7 6 5 4 3 2 1

Design by Linda Carey
Printed in Canada

This book is dedicated to my daughters,
Aki and Michi

List of Characters

Konishi Zenta, a young ronin (wandering samurai)

Ishihara Matsuzo, a friend of Zenta

Itoh Kajiro, another ronin

The old lord, former provincial ruler, now exiled to the island

The commander of the island

Lady Sada, wife of the commander

Lady Yuri, Sada's younger sister

Gorobei, an officer of the island garrison

Abbess, head of the convent

Conspirators

Kimi, maid at an inn on the mainland

Boatman, Kimi's brother

Fisherman and his family

Maids serving the old lord

Chamberlain to the ruling family

Another boatman

Raiko, Yuri's cat

Chapter 1

The skiff was still a little distance from the shore, but the boatman didn't want to go any farther. "The water is only waist deep here," he told his passenger. "You can walk up to the beach easily."

Kajiro clenched his jaw to stop his teeth from chattering. Although his straw cloak protected him from the wind, his skin felt cold and clammy, and his stomach was queasy from the stormy crossing. The trip had taken only an hour, but it felt like several. He wanted shelter, a fire, and hot soup—not a dip in the sea.

"You said you'd take me across," he growled. "And across means all the way across!"

He knew his growl would intimidate no one, for the wind blew away whatever force there was in his voice. But he was a ronin, an unemployed samurai trained for war, and the common people had learned to be wary of ronin, especially a hungry one.

The boatman stole a look at the sky. The sun had risen more than an hour ago, but with the storm clouds pressing heavily down, the morning was still dark. "It'll take too much time to beach the boat and then put it out to sea again," he muttered. "If the storm hits, I may be stranded on the island."

The boatman was clearly afraid. His small eyes showed their whites all around. But which frightened him more, his passenger or the prospect of being stranded on the island? Kajiro could not tell. He opened his straw cloak, exposing the hilts of his two swords. Perhaps the sight of the weapons would persuade the boatman.

But the choice was taken out of their hands. In a sudden swell, the boat shot forward, and it hit the sandy bottom with a jolt that sent the two men tumbling. Kajiro's head cracked against the gunwale. As he struggled to his feet, he suffered less from pain than from humiliation. Slow! His reaction was much too slow. He couldn't blame it on seasickness. It was the months of aimless living, of too much drinking and too little action, except for the sordid brawls that had come his way.

The boatman had fallen forward, and grabbed at the long oar to regain his feet. Another tug of the waves freed the boat, but it was already too late. The sky broke open and rain came pelting down. In seconds the bottom of the boat was filled. Kajiro jumped out and pulled the boat toward shore. "It's no use!" he shouted. "You can't possibly go back to the mainland until the storm is over!"

The boatman didn't need persuading. He joined Kajiro in the water and the two men heaved at the boat. It was quickly becoming heavier, and threatened to pull back into the sea with the undertow.

Although it was late spring, this was the Japan Sea side of the country, bleak and stormy, and the water was biting cold. But the exercise soon warmed them. With a powerful tug, helped by a surge of the waves, they got the boat safely on the beach at last. While the boatman turned the skiff over to empty the water, Kajiro looked around at the shore.

He saw a curved, sandy beach, bounded at either end by craggy rocks. On the beach were a few small fishing boats and some wooden posts, crossbeamed and hung with fishnets. Two open reed huts contained floats, rope, spools, and fish baskets. Farther up on the beach he saw half a dozen fishermen's cottages. It was a small fishing village, but reasonably prosperous—at least that was how it looked through billowing curtains of rain. The island had no other fishing village, for the boatman had said that this small beach was the only harbor. The rest of the island shore was nothing but cliffs and jagged rocks.

The boatman secured his boat and turned to Kajiro. "We'd better find a place where we can dry ourselves," he said glumly. He pointed at a fisherman's cottage. "I know that family over there."

As the two men plodded up the beach, something streaked out from behind one of the huts and zigzagged toward them. In the distance a high voice screamed, "Stop him! Stop him!"

Kajiro reacted instantly: He would not be

caught unprepared this time. Snatching a fish basket hanging in a nearby reed hut, he flung it over the running animal—the beast—whatever it was.

The basket was heavy, but it didn't immobilize the animal for long. Soon the basket began to shake. It crawled forward, bounced, and then crawled forward again. In the gray morning light, the humped, struggling shape looked like nothing Kajiro had seen before. Perhaps a tortoise with an attack of the hiccups came closest. Kajiro wanted to laugh—until he saw the extraordinary reaction of the boatman.

When the boatman turned around and saw the dark, heaving object at his feet, he jumped back and began to shout. "Don't let him get me! Help! Help!"

Was the mysterious animal dangerous after all? Kajiro drew his sword and cautiously circled the shuddering basket.

A savage kick from behind took him on the back of one knee and sent him staggering. He whirled around, sword raised, cursing himself for having been taken off guard—again.

What he saw nearly caused him to drop his sword in surprise. His attacker, now getting ready for another kick, was a slight young boy. No. Kajiro took a closer look at the clothes and the long disheveled hair. It was a girl.

Kajiro quickly sheathed his sword and used his bare hands to hold off his attacker, just as another kick landed painfully on his shin.

"You bullies!" screamed the girl, struggling wildly and continuing to kick viciously. "Two big men like you picking on a poor, helpless animal!"

Kajiro could think of only one thing to do: He picked the girl up and threw her. He heard a splash, and realized that he had thrown harder than he had intended. Good. That would cool her off.

When he looked around, the boatman had stopped bellowing, and was staring down at the basket with a foolish grin on his face. The animal inside was snarling and spitting, but instead of trying to overturn the basket, it was scratching. In fact . . . in fact . . . Kajiro began to laugh when he finally realized what the animal was.

Footsteps squelched behind him, and he whirled around to face the furious girl. Her eyes were blazing, but at least she didn't try to kick him again. Her kimono draped around her in sodden swathes, and on either side of her cheeks, locks of long black hair were plastered like strips of kelp.

"A great big warrior like you, attacking a poor little cat!" she cried. "You should be ashamed of yourself!"

She bent over and lifted the basket. It was indeed a cat inside. For a second, it crouched unmoving, as if mistrusting its freedom. Then it streaked up the front of the girl's kimono and fastened itself on her shoulder. The girl winced, but by patient stroking succeeded in calming the animal and coaxing it into sheathing its claws. "My poor little kitty! My poor darling!"

A poor little kitty was not how Kajiro would describe the animal. He was the fattest cat he had ever seen. He was also the ugliest, now that he had a good look. The girl had smoothed down the wet bedraggled fur, but nothing could improve the cat's face. One eye had a bad squint, probably a fight injury, and the expression on the cat's face was sly and malevolent.

The girl put her cheek against the cat's head and crooned over her baby, her pussikins, her little darling. She would defend him against these big, bad men.

"I was only trying to help," protested Kajiro, stung by her injustice. "You said to stop him, and that's just what I did."

The boatman replaced the fish basket on its shelf. "We're not getting any dryer, standing around in the rain," he grumbled. "Let's get inside that cottage."

The girl looked up from her pet to the cottage, but made no move to rise and follow. She sneezed.

"Your cat is hungry," suggested Kajiro. "You'd better feed him."

Actually, the cat looked as if it could skip several meals and be the healthier for it, but his suggestion did bring the girl quickly to her feet. "Yes, you're right," she said. "Poor kitty, you need your dinner, don't you?"

The windows of the cottage were tightly covered by wooden shutters against the storm. When the boatman asked for admittance, no response came at first. This didn't seem to surprise him. Without raising his voice, he patiently identified himself again and again, and begged for admittance.

Kajiro felt less patient. What was wrong with the fisherman and his family? Even with the noise of the storm, they should have heard the caterwauling outside. Weren't they curious at all?

Finally they heard the wooden crossbar being lifted and the door slid open a crack. An eye peered out. "Oh, it's you," said a voice, and the door opened wider, revealing the nervous face of a local fisherman.

"Who did you think it was?" demanded the boatman. "Come on, let me in. I'm soaked."

When the fisherman saw the ronin, he gasped and tried to close the door again, but the boatman already had a foot in the opening. "It's all right!" he said. "This is a friend. He's going to help us."

Then the fisherman caught sight of the girl with the cat. His mouth fell open. Taking advantage of his surprise, the two drenched men and girl pushed their way into the cottage.

Inside, it was dark, and only a faint reddish light came from the sunken fireplace in the middle of the room. Kajiro heard the scrape of a flint, and a moment later a glow came from a square paper lantern. By its soft yellow light he saw that in addition to the fisherman who had let them in, the cottage contained a gray-haired man and a woman with her arms around two little boys. They all looked terrified.

The cat struggled out of the girl's arms and landed with a thump. The tension broke and one of the boys laughed, "Mamma, look!" he cried. "It's a cat!"

His mother looked at the cat, and then at his mistress. "Lady Yuri!" she gasped. "What are you doing here? You're soaking wet!"

The fisherman and his wife were soon bustling about, drying the girl. While they were finding her a change of clothes, Kajiro and the boatman unlaced their straw sandals, wiped the sand from their feet, and stepped up to the wooden floor of the cottage.

Kajiro realized that he should have known the girl was no villager. Her speech was that of the samurai class, and her kimono was silk. He wondered how old she was. She had felt bony and slight in his hands when he had picked her up earlier.

He sat down near the sunken fireplace and put his long sword down beside him. The fire was down to its embers, but it still gave off a faint warmth, very welcome after the cold and wet. A big iron pot hung from a chain over the fire. He looked wistfully at the curl of steam rising from the pot, which probably contained the family's breakfast. Whatever was simmering inside, was there enough of it to go around?

He noticed the two boys staring at his sword. Perhaps they had never seen a samurai sword at such close quarters before. One of the boys began to stroke the cat, who stretched out near the fire, purring.

Suddenly the cat got up, walked over to Kajiro, and circled him, sniffing. To his amazement, it jumped into his lap and began to lick his hands. He looked at its sly, squinty eyes and realized why the cat was courting him: The basket he had handled earlier had contained some broken pieces of squid, and his hands still smelled of the fish. But he enjoyed the purring and the warm little tongue rasping over his fingers. He had never had an animal as a pet before. Awkwardly he patted the cat's head.

From the far end of the room, partitioned off by a screen, the girl Yuri returned and seated herself at the fire. She wore a borrowed cotton kimono, and her hair was tied in a straight black sheaf down her back. She was older than he had thought at first, probably around fifteen or so. Although she had very fine skin, she was not beautiful. Her face was too thin, and something about the jut of her lower lip promised a stubborn temper.

The fisherman's wife began to ladle food from the iron pot into bowls. She also set out some small dishes of broiled fish. Apologizing for the humble fare and bowing deeply, she served the girl and Kajiro first, and then the boatman and her family. The bowls contained a thick gruel made from yams. It was cheap, plebeian food, but sweet, nourishing, and best of all, hot.

Kajiro finished his portion in a few quick slurps and then looked at the pot. It was now empty. He began to munch on his tiny piece of broiled fish, chewing the crispy head, tail, bones and all. The girl sipped her gruel more slowly, and gave her piece of fish to the cat, who immediately dragged the prize off to a corner, and snarled when one of the boys tried to approach.

As the dishes for the scanty meal were cleared away, the fisherman turned to Kajiro. "Have you come to our island, sir, because you have heard of our ogres?"

Chapter 2

This was the first Kajiro had heard of ogres. Was the fisherman joking?

But nobody in the room was smiling. The two little boys drew closer together and stared at Kajiro with wide eyes. A loud clatter came from the back of the room, where the fisherman's wife was rinsing dishes. She had knocked over a stack of wooden bowls.

Yuri was the first to speak. "Bah! There are no ogres on the island. It's just local superstition. Besides, if there are any ogres, Raiko will take care of them, won't you, Raiko?" She took the cat into her arms and nuzzled him. The cat, with a fishtail sticking out of the corner of his mouth, squirmed a little and rumbled in the back of his throat.

Kajiro suppressed a smile. Raiko was a legendary warrior of the tenth century, renowned for his victory over ogres. It was hard to imagine what he could have in common with this overweight cat.

Now that Raiko had swallowed the rest of his fish, he wriggled out of his mistress's arms and looked around the room. Again he approached Kajiro and sniffed appreciatively at his hands.

The girl looked surprised. "That's funny.

Raiko doesn't usually like strangers." Perhaps influenced by the attitude of her cat, she became less hostile. "Who are you?" she asked Kajiro. "You're not an islander."

"He's a famous samurai!" said the boatman, before the ronin could speak. "He's renowned for his courage and his swordsmanship!"

Kajiro was embarrassed. While negotiating on the mainland about the crossing, he had noticed that the boatman was treating him with unusual respect. Indeed, the man's deference seemed so exaggerated that Kajiro had wondered briefly if the boatman was being ironical. It puzzled him, and he finally put it down to the awe that some commoners had for members of the samurai class. Now he began to wonder. Was it possible that he was being mistaken for someone else? Someone who really was notable for his swordsmanship?

If that was the case, there might be more embarrassment in store. On the other hand, Kajiro needed an excuse for coming to the island. He thought back to his interview on the mainland with the chamberlain, the second most powerful man in the province, next to the daimyo himself. "Your mission is to go to the island and keep your eyes on the commander of the garrison there," the chamberlain had said. "You must do it without revealing that you are a spy in my pay. And if you see the least sign that there is something suspicious, you must find means to report back to me immediately."

Well, if the islanders mistook him for a famous warrior who was here to probe the mystery of the ogres, Kajiro would do nothing to correct their error. He turned to his host. "Do you really believe in the ogres?"

The fisherman dropped his eyes. "I'm not the only one who believes in them," he muttered.

"Tell me about the ogres," said Kajiro. "Have they always been a menace here?"

"Our island has been plagued by ogres for as long as people remember," replied the fisherman.

Kajiro knew that such stories were especially common in coastal villages or on islands, although they could appear in all parts of the country. Many children's fairy tales contained stories about ogres, or *oni*. During the festival of Setsubun, regular "ogre chasing" rites were performed, when beans were thrown to get rid of them. The actor playing the part of an ogre was always made up with huge, round eyes, and wore a wig of curly hair, which was often colored red or yellow.

For himself, Kajiro believed that the so-called ogres were probably shipwrecked sailors from some faraway country inhabited by people with deep round eyes and light-colored hair. He himself had met a few of the foreigners and found them not nearly so grotesque as reported, although he had seen one or two with reddish hair. In recent years, large numbers of them had come from a country called Portugal to trade and to preach their religion, called Christianity. While their behavior was alien, it could not be described as completely uncivilized. But perhaps to an isolated fishing village, anyone looking so different would seem like a freak, an ogre.

Kajiro was still puzzled, however. "If you've always had ogre stories here on the island, why are you particularly concerned now? Has something happened recently?"

For a moment no one spoke. Then the fisherman's wife rose. "Go and play in the corner," she told her sons. "Don't bother the grown-ups."

The two boys were dragged away protesting. Their mother opened a cupboard and took out some toys—a couple of wooden tops and some small animal figures woven from rice straw. Then she placed the folding screen in front of the boys, cutting them off from view. Soon, however, Kajiro caught sight of two small heads poking out, one from either end of the screen.

When the fisherman spoke again, his voice was lower. "For the past few weeks, things have been disappearing here on the island," he told the ronin.

Theft, of course, thought Kajiro. It was uncommon in a small, close-knit community, but not unheard of. "What sort of things were taken?" he asked. "Household utensils? Clothing?"

The fisherman shook his head. "Animals. We've been losing animals. Several of the farmers on the island have lost chickens."

"Foxes, maybe?" suggested Kajiro. They were the most likely to carry off chickens.

The fisherman shook his head. "Our island isn't big enough to support foxes, or any other large predator animals."

"How about a hawk or an eagle, then?" asked Kajiro. "Some of those birds are quite powerful, and can carry off a chicken."

Again the fisherman shook his head. "A chicken, perhaps, but not a dog."

Kajiro felt a chill on his neck. "You mean . . ."

"Yes," the fisherman said softly, "some of the farmers on the island have lost their watchdogs."

Kajiro tried to laugh. "Maybe the dogs carried off the chickens, and the owners of the chickens killed the dogs to get even."

"The farmers insisted that their dogs would never kill chickens," said the fisherman. "They were carefully trained to guard them."

Ogres were not just fairy tales to these people. Kajiro began to understand his boatman's reluctance to be stranded here. No wonder the man had been so alarmed by the sight of the shaking basket with Raiko trapped inside, if he thought he was on an island of ogres.

The gray-haired grandfather began to speak. "The ogres are demanding sacrifices." His voice had a singsong lilt, as if he was reciting a ballad. "In the time of our ancestors, regular sacrifices were made to appease the ogres."

23

"Raiko!" the girl suddenly cried. "Where is Raiko?"

"He's here, next to me," said Kajiro. The cat had finished washing his face and was turning about, trying to find a comfortable position for sleep.

As the girl snatched up her cat, Kajiro looked around helplessly at the fisherman's family. "I'm not sure what I can do. . . ."

"*You* will be able to defeat the ogres, if anyone can!" interrupted the boatman. "Didn't you once destroy a vampire cat that was murdering all the girls in some village up north?"

Now Kajiro knew for sure that the boatman had mistaken him for someone else. Who could it be? He hoped that the islanders wouldn't expect some spectacular display of swordsmanship from him. He was in no condition to oblige them.

Even the girl looked impressed by the boatman's words. "Is it really true, what he said about the vampire cat?"

Kajiro couldn't meet her eyes. "Well, you see . . ."

At that moment a loud voice began shouting outside. "Open up! We know you're in there!"

Trembling, the fisherman hastened to open the door. Standing outside, with droplets of rain running down their wide-brimmed lacquered hats, were a dozen soldiers. Their officer stepped forward and signaled his men to form a semicircle about the door. "Come out!" he shouted again. "It's no use! You can't escape."

"This is insufferable!" hissed the girl, jumping to her feet. Her face turned crimson with fury. Stalking to the entrance she faced the soldiers. "How dare you speak to me like that?"

At the sight of the girl, the officer looked stunned. "L-Lady Yuri! I didn't know it was you in there!"

Yuri glared at him. "So it's you, Gorobei. I thought I recognized that arrogant voice. What were you yelling about?"

The officer called Gorobei bowed. "One of our men patrolling the harbor reported that a boat landed here with a stranger aboard. As you know, all strangers arriving on the island have to be taken into custody and questioned."

Kajiro knew it was time to show his face. "I believe you are looking for me?" he asked the officer.

The soldiers instantly formed a tighter ring, and several men put their hands on their swords. Gorobei looked at the ronin grimly. "You are under arrest, and also the boatman who brought you here."

"Don't be ridiculous!" snapped Yuri. "This gentleman came here to find out who's been stealing all the animals. Since you haven't done much to solve the mystery, you should be grateful for his help."

Her words were obviously calculated to

sting, but Gorobei showed no emotion. "Never-theless, we must question all strangers, espe-cially those who come here unannounced."

"W-We m-meant to announce ourselves immediately!" protested the boatman. "I swear that's the truth! But after we landed, it started p-pouring, and then that cat came running, and the young lady chased the cat and . . . well . . . things happened. We all got wet, so we came in here to dry off . . . the young lady, too."

As the boatman stammered out his expla-nations, some of the men relaxed, and one or two were seen to suppress smiles. Even the offi-cer's face gradually lost its harshness. "Yes, well, things usually happen when the young lady chases her cat," he said.

He turned to Yuri. "Does your sister know you're here?"

Yuri's lower lip jutted out. "I didn't see any reason to bother Sada when I was just going out to look for Raiko. I knew he liked to hang around the fishing boats, so I came here to look for him."

"Lady Sada will be very worried," Gorobei pointed out.

Yuri bridled. "Sada's just my sister, not my mother!"

"Lady Sada is also your guardian, and responsible for your safety," Gorobei explained patiently.

As Kajiro listened to the exchange between the officer and the girl, he decided it wasn't the first clash between the two. Yuri's lower lip not only protruded, it was trembling with annoyance. Gorobei, for his part, was obviously making a strong effort to control his exasperation.

Finally Gorobei said, "We're simply wasting time standing here arguing." At his signal, the soldiers closed in on the ronin and the boatman.

"There's no need to treat these men like criminals!" cried Yuri. "They're friends! They helped me catch Raiko!"

"A sure sign that they are valiant men and true," agreed Gorobei dryly. "But they still have to come and explain themselves."

Their destination was the mansion where the soldiers of the island and their commander had their headquarters. At least it had stopped raining, thought the ronin, as they plodded along in a double file. Away from the beach the ground was muddy from the storm and sucked at their feet. One of the soldiers suggested carrying the girl on his back, but she rejected his offer with a toss of her head.

She did, however, allow the ronin to carry Raiko, who seemed to be rapidly gaining weight with every step. But Kajiro enjoyed carrying the cat. Although he knew it could perfectly well take care of itself, he felt protective.

The island was small, replied one of the soldiers when Kajiro asked about its size. In addition to the fishing village it supported about a dozen farm families, who sold vegetables and eggs to the mansion. But the soil was too poor for growing rice, which had to be brought over from the mainland.

Kajiro learned that the island also had a convent with some fifteen nuns in residence. The women were from good families on the mainland, although the abbess was a relative of Lady Yuri's family and an islander. As strict vegetarians, the nuns ate neither fish nor eggs. Except for buying a few vegetables, they stayed independent of the island's economy.

The mansion was the largest building on the island, said the soldier, for it housed the commander, his family, various attendants, and the soldiers of the garrison. The ronin was surprised that a garrison was on the island at all, if it was so small and so sparsely populated. When he asked how many men were stationed there, the soldier fell silent and stared suspiciously at him.

They soon passed the farm village. It consisted of a few houses set close together, each with a shed containing tools, carts, and some poultry cages. Close by were vegetable plots of modest sizes. The clouds had lifted at last, and the rays of the morning sun shed a yellow light on the worn thatched roofs and shabby mud walls of the farmhouses. Kajiro thought that while the fishermen were doing well enough, the farmers seemed to be having a hard time making a living on the island's stony soil. They couldn't afford to lose any of their animals. The chickens, especially, produced not only eggs but droppings, which must have been a vital source of fertilizer.

After they passed the farm village, a short march took them to the mansion. It was situated at the highest point and commanded a view over most of the island. Looking back, Kajiro could see the slight dip where the farmhouses were. Beyond it he made out the curve of the fishing village with its bay, which had been grayish green earlier, but was now a clear blue in the sunlight. From the soldiers Kajiro gathered that the convent was on the other side of the mansion, above a sheer cliff close to the edge of the sea.

The mansion was large and solidly built. It was surrounded by a high, stone-based wall of mud brick, plastered over and covered on top with dark-gray tiles. The roofs of the buildings showing above the wall were also tiled in dark gray. Around the edges of the roofs were round, decorative tiles stamped with a family crest. It was the crest of the daimyo who ruled the whole province, which included not only the island, but a portion of the coastal mainland. This mansion was not a private residence: It was a military fortress belonging to the daimyo on the mainland.

Kajiro was sorry he had not listened more carefully to talk about the political situation of the region. He did know, however, that the ruling clan was headed by the vigorous and able young daimyo, a warlord who had assumed power two years earlier after his father had abdicated because of ill health. Perhaps the island was an important outpost for the defense of his domain against a seaborne invasion. In this age of civil wars, one never knew when a rival warlord from some neighboring province could be planning an attack.

The party was not admitted through the gates without challenge. If the island was really a military outpost, the tight security would not be surprising. Once inside the well-guarded gates, the party crossed an immaculately raked courtyard of white sand, decorated with mounds of moss and smoothly sheared bushes. At the far end of the courtyard, they stepped up to a covered walk.

Halfway down the walk, a sliding screen opened and an elderly serving woman emerged. On seeing Yuri, the woman broke into a noisy gabble. "Lady Yuri! What happened? Where did you get that shabby kimono?"

Yuri refused to follow the woman and change into more suitable clothes. She insisted on accompanying the party to the audience chamber, to make sure, she said, that there would be no "misunderstanding" about the strangers.

Kajiro was touched by Yuri's support. But he suspected that her support would last only as long as Raiko showed a liking for him. He hurriedly scratched the cat under the chin, and was rewarded by a rumbling purr.

At the door of the audience chamber, Gorobei stopped and announced their arrival.

The room was large and divided into two parts: the front part had a floor of dark, polished wood, and a smaller back part was slightly raised and covered with tatami mats. Along the back wall was a folding screen, with a large painting of an aged cherry tree against a bold background of silver and green. The island commander and his wife were seated on the raised portion of the room, in front of the screen.

"Commander, Lady Sada," said the officer, bowing deeply. "Here are the strangers."

Kajiro, the boatman, and their escort all bowed and waited in the wooden corridor outside the room. Yuri entered and sat down on a flat, square cushion to one side of her sister. She looked defiant.

Lady Sada seemed about five years older than Yuri. While the family resemblance between the two girls was strong, the older sister's face was not so thin and much prettier, even beautiful. She had the same jutting lower lip as Yuri, but her maturer features showed more than just childish stubbornness: they showed a formidable will.

Next to Lady Sada was the commander, her husband. He was a youngish man and handsome, with a good muscular build. Unlike his wife, he seemed detached from the proceedings, and his eyes were wide and limpid, like the eyes of a child or an idiot. Why had the young daimyo appointed such an absentminded man to the command of this important island? Was he really absentminded? It was Kajiro's task to find out.

Lady Sada began the questioning. "What have we here? Castaways?"

The boatman hurriedly muttered something about the storm. Lady Sada nodded carelessly and looked at Kajiro. "So. While innocently fishing off the coast, you were blown to our island by the storm?"

Kajiro found it difficult to execute a graceful bow with a cat on his lap. But when he started to lift Raiko, the cat dug his claws in and his squinty eyes flashed a warning at him.

Lady Sada was still waiting for an answer. She looked amused rather than impatient, however. Kajiro tried to think of a plausible reason for his visit to the island, and suddenly he remembered what the fisherman in the cottage had said. "Lady Sada," he began, "I heard reports that this island was troubled by ogres."

He sensed a stirring among the soldiers on either side of him. Of the people present, only the commander looked wholly unconcerned.

Lady Sada smiled. "So you've come to help us? You have some plan for destroying the ogres?"

"*Somebody* is responsible for stealing the animals," Yuri broke in. "This gentleman will solve the problem for us. He once defeated a vampire cat!"

For a moment Lady Sada looked startled.

Then she smiled again, more widely than before. "My, I didn't know we had such a courageous champion with us! Can you tell me the name of this gentleman who has come to save us from the ogres?"

Kajiro felt his face reddening. He was conscious of his unkempt appearance, but even more of his slack condition, which must be obvious to Lady Sada's keen eyes.

The boatman was unable to keep silent any longer. "He is a famous warrior! His name is Konishi Zenta!"

Zenta! So that was the man he was being mistaken for! Kajiro barely suppressed a gasp of dismay. He knew of Zenta's reputation, and he had heard some talk on the mainland that the man was being expected. In his present state, could he possibly pass himself off as this renowned warrior? What if the real Zenta arrived? As these thoughts whirled through his head, he looked up nervously at Lady Sada for her reaction.

She broke out into peals of laughter.

Chapter 3

Sada was still chuckling when she left the audience chamber. The ronin might be able to impress the local fishermen and farmers, and convince them that he was a noted warrior—Konishi Zenta, no less. To be sure, he was not bad-looking. He was above average in height, with good shoulders and the sinewy wrists of a practiced swordsman.

But did he really expect that his condition would fool experienced eyes? Although he seemed no older than twenty-five or so, his face was already slack, a sign of too much drinking and too little exercise. Nor had she missed the sluggishness of his movements and the faint tremor in his hands. True, the tremor probably indicated that he had not had a recent drink, but it showed he desperately needed one.

Then why hadn't she ordered his expulsion? Why had she offered him freedom and the hospitality of the garrison? She was still a little surprised at herself. Perhaps . . . perhaps it was because there was something honest and direct in his face, despite his preposterous claims.

At least her morning had started on a light note for a change. But now she had to face an unpleasant duty: her morning visit to her prisoner, the former daimyo. She had been visiting the old lord daily, ever since he had been exiled to the island. She hated these visits. It was not merely because the prisoner was mad. Sada had an old nursemaid in her seventies whose mind had begun to wander, but the old woman remained a gentle, contented soul, crooning children's songs to herself and always greeting her visitors with a happy smile.

Sada's prisoner, on the other hand, also greeted his visitors with a smile, but it was different. His smile hinted that he had secrets, important and unpleasant secrets.

Sada admitted that her discomfort had another reason. The old lord had once been the daimyo, the ruler of the province. When his unstable mental condition had become evident, he had been legitimately deposed by a council of elders and replaced by his son. All the steps had been taken with the proper formalities and in accordance with the principles set down by their ancestors.

Yet Sada could not help feeling like a traitor in mounting guard over the exile. She and her family had sworn undying loyalty to the old man, after all. Once her husband, with surprising thoughtfulness, had offered to visit the prisoner in her place. But Sada had refused. He was not observant enough, and he might not notice subtle changes in the exile's condition, changes that had to be reported to the young daimyo. She had another reason. Her father, being without sons, had followed the usual practice of adopting his son-in-law as his heir. But though Sada's husband had become commander after her father's death, she took full responsibility for guarding the exile. She did not expect her husband, an adopted son, to have the same sense of duty.

At the door leading to the exile's suite of rooms, the guard saluted Sada and reported that the old lord was now quiet, although he had been talking loudly earlier in the morning.

Sada frowned. The ranting was a recent development, begun only a few days ago. If it became worse, she would have to report it to the mainland. "Send the two serving women out to me," she said. "I want to question them first before seeing the old lord."

The two maids, girls in their late teens, bowed deeply and waited to be questioned. Sada had chosen them for their good nature and patience. They had to be able to tolerate behavior from the old lord that was whimsical, eccentric, or even bizarre. One girl was very pretty and vivacious, while the other one was no less good-looking but quiet. The former daimyo might be exiled to the island, but he was still entitled to attractive and attentive serving girls.

"I understand that the old lord has been shouting again," said Sada. "What sort of things has he been saying? Could you understand him?"

The talkative girl raised her head. "Oh, my lady, he has been talking about the ogres! He claims they are his friends, and they've come because he sent for them!"

Sada tried to hide her dismay. Stories about ogres had always circulated among the island people, but with the disappearance of the animals, they had begun to affect the morale of the garrison. The soldiers might protest loudly that they didn't believe in children's stories, but Sada could detect an increasing nervousness in her men. The old lord's ranting was not going to help.

"Did either of you mention the disappearance of the animals to the old lord?" she asked the maids.

"Oh no, my lady, of course not!" protested the talkative maid. Her silent companion's answer was a shake of the head.

"Very well," sighed Sada. Even if they had mentioned the animals, they wouldn't admit it now. "Wait for me outside."

When Sada entered the old lord's chamber, he was gazing at a picture scroll hanging in an alcove. He turned his head as she sank into a deep, reverential bow. After murmuring the proper greeting, she raised her eyes and forced herself to meet his gaze. It was difficult, although he was only a helpless old man and she held all the power on the island.

He was still a strikingly handsome man, with strongly molded features, sharpened, not blurred, by age. His bearing was dignified and in keeping with his former exalted position.

His eyes were bright, mischievous, and quite mad.

Sada asked the usual questions about his health, his food, and whether the maids had been properly attentive.

As always, the old lord replied that everything had been satisfactory. Then, in a calm and reasonable voice, he said, "But I may need more animals for my friends, the ogres."

Despite herself Sada blinked. "M-More animals, my lord?"

"Yes," said the old lord. His eyes sparkled merrily. "They don't eat like us, you know. They want to eat red meat, not just chickens."

Sada tried to show nothing but polite interest. "They told you they wanted the animals, my lord?"

The old lord beamed. "Oh yes, two of the ogres visited me last night, a tall one and a short one. The short one had tall horns, and the tall one had short horns." He began to giggle.

"I . . . I will see what I can do," said Sada. She was not quite able to keep her voice steady.

"You'd better do something soon," said the old lord, as Sada rose to leave. "The ogres have taken several dogs already. They may start on people next—a young child from the village, for instance." He was still giggling when she left the room.

Sada knew that her sick disgust showed on her face. One of the guards outside grinned at her. "Eerie, isn't he?"

"Don't be impertinent!" Sada said sharply. "All due respect must be shown to the old lord!"

Nevertheless, she knew how the guards felt, what they had to listen to hour after hour. She made a note to rotate the men more frequently, so that each spell of duty became shorter.

A sudden thought struck her. "Has anyone been in to see the old lord last night?"

The guard shook his head. "No one is admitted without your explicit permission, my lady. We do a daily search of the rooms, of course, to check that no unauthorized person can hide in there."

She nodded approval at the guard, but as she turned away, she was still uneasy. How had the exile learned about the disappearing animals? His knowledge even extended to the watchdogs. She decided that he must have heard about the dogs from one of the maids, the talkative one. It was too late to replace the girl now, for the damage was already done. Besides, the girl with her sunny, uncomplaining nature had a soothing effect on the mad old man.

Now Sada had another visit to make, a much pleasanter one. She was going to that wing of the mansion where her guest was installed. He was *her* guest, *her* friend, not her husband's. When the animals had started disappearing and the rumors became troublesome, she had sent for him. He had come at her bidding, but now he was ill. He would be too weak to be of any use in the coming days, days that could be crucial.

At the door of the guest's room, Sada met the physician. "How is he?" she asked.

"The fever has broken," replied the physician. "Now it's just a matter of quiet and rest. Make sure he drinks plenty of liquids. As for food, a thin rice gruel is good, but it should be lukewarm."

Some of Sada's anxiety lifted. "How long will it take him to regain his strength?"

"He could probably be on his feet again in a week—sooner, if he's careful," said the physician. He shook his head warningly. "He should avoid any strenuous activity, or the fever may return."

A week, thought Sada. That's too long. She might not have that much time. According to the reports she had received, the attempt to rescue the old daimyo would be made very soon.

She pushed open the sliding door and entered. A serving girl was putting away the damp cloths used to cool the patient's head. At Sada's nod, the girl bowed and left the room.

Sada sat down on the floor by the patient's bedside and looked down at him. He had lost his hectic flush and was now pale. Examining his features, she saw all the things that she had searched for in her husband's face but had never found. Here she could see determination and strength of purpose, and most of all, self-confidence. If only . . . if only . . . She was twenty-one years old, and her life was a series of disappointments.

The guest opened his eyes. "I haven't been very helpful so far, have I?" His voice was clear, and stronger than Sada had expected. She felt a return of hope.

"Has anything been happening?" he asked.

"A few more chickens have disappeared," she said. "Wait, you haven't heard about the latest. Some of the villagers have lost their watchdogs. We combed the whole island without discovering a single trace of the animals."

The guest frowned. After a moment he asked, "How is the old lord? Is he more troublesome than before?"

"He shouts sometimes," said Sada. "Just now he told me that the island ogres took the animals, and that two of them came to visit him last night—a tall one and a short one."

"How did he hear about the animals disappearing?" asked the guest. His voice had risen, and he sounded agitated.

Sada was sorry she had mentioned the ogres. "One of the maids must have been talking. You know how girls can chatter. Why didn't the ogres snatch that chatterbox instead? We can spare her more than chickens or watchdogs!"

The guest smiled faintly and relaxed, closing his eyes again. "What about your husband? Is he doing anything about the ogre rumors?"

As always, when her husband was mentioned, Sada felt irritation rise in her, like bile. "If he's doing anything, he's not telling me about it. Frankly, I think he's too busy writing poetry to bother."

"Do you think the ogre business is connected with the conspiracy to rescue the exile and restore him to power?" asked the guest.

"I have a feeling in my bones that it is," Sada said slowly. "But I don't see how."

The guest stirred restlessly. "It must be connected!"

Sada saw that she was tiring him, and she rose to leave. At the door she paused. "By the way, this may amuse you. A ronin arrived on the island this morning, a scruffy-looking vagabond. He claims he's the famous warrior Konishi Zenta!"

"I wonder what the man is hoping to do on the island," murmured the guest. "Does he look dangerous?"

Sada laughed. "Dangerous? He's so out of condition that he's not up to fighting Yuri's cat!"

"A good swordsman, even if out of condition, can be dangerous," said the guest. "And he can work himself back into condition, given the will to do it."

"Don't worry," Sada said lightly. "I really do believe that he's harmless. He might even help. He says he has come to hunt for ogres. Besides, Yuri approves of him."

The guest smiled. "You accept him because of Yuri's recommendation?"

Sada did not answer at first. "You know, I think I do," she said finally. So that was what had decided her. Without realizing, she had been influenced by her younger sister's judgment on the ronin. "She's no fool, Yuri," Sada said thoughtfully. "She may act like a child, but she's not stupid."

"Nobody in your family is stupid," said the guest.

"Well, if Yuri likes this ronin, I'm prepared to let him scour the island for ogres," said Sada.

As she began to slide open the door, the guest asked, "Does your ronin mention a young companion of his, called Matsuzo?"

"No," said Sada. "He said nothing about Matsuzo. He came alone."

Matsuzo had not come to the island. He was still in the mainland coastal town. At the moment, he was extremely uncomfortable. But he was not seriously worried, not at first. His captors had tied him to a post in one of the rooms at the inn, but they never failed to untie him for meals and calls of nature. Short of letting him go, they were always polite, even considerate. The food they brought him was the best the inn had to offer, better than what he and Zenta had eaten when they were by themselves.

Zenta—that was his main concern. Where was Zenta? During the clash with the men who had captured him, he had lost sight of his friend. Obviously Zenta had escaped. Matsuzo tried putting himself in his friend's place. What would he be likely to do? Stage a rescue, of course. Perhaps Zenta thought the odds too unfavorable for a successful rescue, and had gone for help. Why was he taking so long? The only answer that occurred to Matsuzo was that Zenta didn't trust the people in this coastal town, and had gone inland to the daimyo's capital for more men.

But it was not like Zenta to look for help. He usually relied on his ingenuity for some sort of trick when the odds looked unfavorable. Matsuzo was baffled by Zenta's long absence.

Even more baffling was his own imprisonment. What did his captors want? They had attacked him and Zenta without warning, and then they had gone to some trouble and expense to keep him captive at this inn. Thinking at the first that they were officers of the daimyo, he had protested with courtesy and dignity that he had no hostile intentions toward the ruling clan, and was perfectly ready to submit to questioning by the authorities.

With equal courtesy his captors responded that they were not accusing him of any crime. They merely wanted to know what his plans were. The man who looked like the leader of his guards questioned him most intently. What was he doing in this coastal town? Was he planning to go to the island? And hadn't he been traveling with a companion?

All the men Matsuzo had seen so far were well dressed and well-spoken—not bandits who kidnapped passing travelers. They appeared to be respectable samurai of the ruling clan. Then why didn't they march him off to the castle town for questioning?

It wasn't until the second day that Matsuzo realized what his guards wanted: They wanted to recruit him. Or rather, they were trying to recruit him and Zenta both. That was the reason for their searching questions about his background and his traveling companion.

On one of his trips to the toilet, he saw Kimi, a maid at the inn. When he and Zenta had first arrived at the inn, Kimi had been their serving girl and she had gone out of her way to be attentive. In happier circumstances, Matsuzo felt he and the girl could have become friends—very good friends. He liked her eyes, which were full of laughter even when the rest of her face was demure. But now the laughter was gone. When she saw the red welts on his arms left by the rope, she winced and her eyes filled with tears.

Back in his room Matsuzo saw that his captors had been joined by a newcomer, someone who had traveled hard and fast, by the looks of his dusty, sweat-stained clothes. The newcomer and one of the guards had been talking together in a low voice, and when Matsuzo entered, they broke off their conversation.

The newcomer looked searchingly at the young ronin. All of Matsuzo's captors so far looked like respectable samurai, but the newcomer was something more. He looked like a man who was used to giving orders and having them promptly obeyed. He had very close-set eyes, as if they were connected under the bridge of his nose. They were compelling eyes. After a silent examination, the newcomer spoke abruptly. "Why have you come here?"

Matsuzo sighed and gave the same answer he had given several times before. "I'm looking for work. What ronin isn't, these days?"

"Yes, but why here, particularly?" asked the newcomer. "Have you heard something about this locality? Did someone tell you there was work to be found here?"

"My friend was the one who decided to come," admitted Matsuzo. "He thought he could find a position here."

"Where is your friend?" demanded the newcomer.

"He escaped during the fighting at the harbor," said Matsuzo. "I don't know where he is now."

The newcomer and the guard exchanged glances. "We've been watching the main roads out of the town," said the guard. "Nobody has reported seeing him."

"And he's not at the castle town," said the newcomer. "I've just come from there, and I didn't see him."

They're as mystified by Zenta's disappearance as I am, thought Matsuzo. But it was a small satisfaction.

The newcomer started to speak again, but fell silent when Kimi appeared with trays of food. Matsuzo noticed that her movements were stiff and jerky, and that she kept her eyes lowered. He realized she was very frightened.

While the maid was arranging the food trays and filling the rice bowls, the newcomer left to wash himself. He was obviously a man of fastidious habits, not a hungry ronin ready to pounce on the food as soon as it was set before him. When he returned, the three men began to eat. The room was quiet except for the faint swish of Kimi's kimono as she moved around, refilling rice bowls and cups.

Normally, Matsuzo had a keen appreciation of good food. But this time he could only pick at the succulent baby abalone, a specialty of the region. The forced inactivity of the past two days, added to his anxiety over Zenta, had robbed him of his appetite. After only one bowl of rice, helped down with some salted eggplant pickles, he put down his chopsticks and sat back. Kimi offered more wine, but Matsuzo refused, putting his hand over his cup. It was tempting to calm his nerves by some drinking, but he needed to keep his head clear.

Kimi seemed to be less attentive than usual. She started to pour despite Matsuzo's refusal, and some of the hot wine spilled on the back of his hand. As he hissed and drew back his hand, the girl began to apologize profusely. Taking a small cloth from her sash, she insisted on wiping his hand and wrist, gingerly touching the skin and asking if the burn was painful.

The wine was not hot enough to cause real pain, but as Matsuzo started to say so, he felt the girl's fingers tap warningly on his wrist. An instant later, a small piece of folded paper was pressed against his palm. Quickly closing his fist over the paper, he frowned at the girl. "Stop fussing! Just be more careful next time!"

Kimi bowed humbly, moved away, and busied herself serving the other guests. While they were holding out their wine cups to be refilled, Matsuzo quickly thrust the note into his sleeve. He would have to find an opportunity later to read it.

After the dinner was over, Kimi cleared away the dishes and left the room. The newcomer turned his close-set eyes back to Matsuzo. "Your friend is Konishi Zenta, isn't he?"

Still wondering how he could find an opportunity to read Kimi's note, Matsuzo didn't immediately reply.

"Don't bother to deny it," said the newcomer. "I've been questioning the inn servants, and you were overheard addressing him by that name."

Since denial was useless, Matsuzo nodded. "Yes, that is my friend's name. We came to look for honest work, the two of us. Since you appear to be familiar with Zenta's reputation, you must know that he would never do anything dishonorable."

The answer seemed to satisfy the newcomer. "We are fully aware of Zenta's character. That is why we are prepared to offer him—and you as well—employment in our enterprise."

The other samurai, the guard, agreed. "From what we saw of your fighting skills, I'm convinced we can use your services."

"The fight was an unfortunate misunderstanding," said the newcomer, frowning at the guard. "You blundered there. Why didn't you explain to Zenta what you wanted?"

"He didn't give us a chance," muttered the other man. "Somehow he decided we were hostile, and after a brief struggle he disappeared."

"He may still be in the vicinity," said the newcomer thoughtfully. "Perhaps he's looking for a boat to take him across to the island. I think we'd better keep a close watch on all the boatmen in the harbor."

"We can't make it too obvious that we're patrolling the beach," said the guard.

That was when Matsuzo finally understood. How could he have been so stupid? Because his captors dressed well and had gentlemanly manners, he had assumed they were men of good standing among the local ruling clan. What he should have noticed was the secrecy, the furtiveness of his captors. They always stopped talking when the innkeeper or one of the serving girls was present. They did not dare patrol the beach or search for Zenta too openly.

The conclusion should have been obvious. These men might be respectable samurai, but they were not supporters of the young daimyo. Matsuzo was now positive that his captors were secret plotters. The newcomer, with his air of command, was obviously some person of rank. This meant that the conspiracy was more than a circle of disgruntled underlings. This was a major attempt to topple the regime of the present daimyo.

Later, when he had been tied to the pillar again, Matsuzo examined his prospects. The conspirators wanted to hire good swordsmen, and had hinted that they were ready to pay well and even offer permanent positions once they assumed power. Matsuzo didn't have to be told that they would kill him if he refused their offer. He knew too much.

Could he pretend to accept their offer? He was still a samurai, and if he pledged himself to join the conspiracy, he would have to keep his word. Would Zenta approve if he joined? Matsuzo doubted it. Although Zenta had not gone into detail about the political situation of the province, he had given the impression that he approved of the young daimyo who was the new head of the clan.

Matsuzo tried to compose himself for sleep, but it was difficult. He knew that the only thing he could do was stall for time—look indecisive, act stupid, do anything but give a definite answer to his captors. But time was what the conspirators did not have, and they already looked as if they were becoming impatient. If

Zenta didn't come to the rescue soon, it might be too late for Matsuzo.

Kimi's note was his only hope. He guessed that it contained some words of support, perhaps even a message from Zenta. What he had to do was find opportunity to take it out and read it unobserved.

Chapter 4

In the afternoon Lady Sada told Kajiro that he was no longer under suspicion. Apparently she was ready to accept him as Konishi Zenta, which rather surprised him. He had not forgotten her mocking laughter that morning. Whether her husband, the commander, accepted the imposture wasn't clear. But it didn't seem to matter. Kajiro had already discovered that on the island, Lady Sada was the one the men obeyed.

Kajiro's second audience with Lady Sada was held in a smaller room, which opened out into a charming garden. On the ground several kinds of moss formed a patchwork of different greens, while a late-blooming azalea provided splashes of red. After the storm the air was clean, and the moisture left on the moss by the rain sparkled with sharp little points of light.

Lady Sada's manner was more gracious than it had been during his first interview. In the bright midday light Kajiro could see her face more clearly, and it looked careworn. There were faint smudges under her eyes, and two tiny lines appeared on either side of her mouth when she tightened her lips. Unlike Yuri, whose face had a certain buoyancy even when she looked stubborn, Lady Sada showed unmistakable signs of discontent. In forty years she might become a very crabby old woman, thought Kajiro. He couldn't help contrasting her face with that of the commander's smooth, carefree countenance.

"Are you still planning to search the island?" asked Lady Sada. "Our soldiers have already looked everywhere, you know."

The soldiers he had seen so far appeared to be efficient. They had probably looked under every stone and behind every tree. It was unlikely that they would miss any hiding place. A big watchdog, after all, was hard to overlook. Nevertheless, Kajiro was intrigued by the mystery, and also by the stories about the ogres. It suited his purpose to look around the island.

He bowed. "With your permission, Lady Sada, I should like to search the island a little."

Lady Sada rose. "Very well, then, you have leave to make a search. If you find a trace of the missing animals, you won't forget to let us know, will you?"

She still didn't take him seriously, thought Kajiro. He couldn't blame her, for he knew perfectly well that her sharp eyes had noticed his poor condition. A spy didn't have to be in superb fighting condition, he thought bitterly. As he moved across the front courtyard toward the gate, he thought about the surprising change in his status. Earlier that morning he had been a suspicious stranger, brought in under guard for questioning. This afternoon he was free to roam wherever he wanted.

He soon discovered that he was not as free as he had thought. Waiting for him at the gate was Gorobei, the officer who had arrested him that morning. "The commander was afraid you might get lost," the officer informed him blandly. "His orders are for me to show you around."

"The commander's orders, or Lady Sada's?" Kajiro could not resist asking.

The officer laughed. He had faint lines on his forehead, which made him look close to thirty. When he laughed, however, the lines disappeared, and Kajiro guessed he was much younger. At lunch the ronin had noticed that Gorobei was well liked by the men. He might have a sure touch with the men under him, but it seemed to fail with Yuri. Toward the girl, he was like a patient adult making allowances for a spoiled child. Kajiro did not consider himself an expert on girls, but he could have told Gorobei that this was the worst possible manner to adopt toward Yuri.

"Actually there's a good reason for me to join you in the search," said Gorobei as he pushed open the gate.

"Aside from keeping an eye on me?" asked Kajiro.

Gorobei grinned. "Aside from keeping an eye on you. I grew up on this island. I know my way around, and I can show you some shortcuts that will save you time."

Kajiro was delighted. Here was the perfect person to tell him about the ogres. Unlike the superstitious fishermen, Gorobei wouldn't be frightened at being questioned.

"Do the people here really believe in ogres?" asked Kajiro.

"Oh yes, we believe in ogres," said the officer readily. "We've always had them, and we have to be careful not to do anything to offend them." He was smiling as he said it, however, and Kajiro could not decide whether he was serious.

As the two men stepped outside the gate, the officer's smile faded. Waiting for them, a bamboo basket in hand, was Yuri.

Gorobei did not look pleased. "Lady Yuri! What are you doing here?"

Yuri's manner was casual. "I've decided to join your search. Raiko will be handy if you run across any ogres."

At that moment the basket shook and a paw reached out between two slats.

Gorobei took a deep breath. The lines on his forehead reappeared, giving him again his old-young look. "Tramping all over the island is not suitable for a young lady, especially carrying that monster of a cat."

"Zenta can carry Raiko," Yuri said. She turned and looked meltingly at Kajiro. "You will, won't you? Raiko likes you. I've never seen him take to anyone so quickly before."

Her use of the name Zenta made Kajiro uncomfortable, but he was flattered to be told that Raiko liked him. Meekly he took the cat's basket. Raiko seemed to signal his approval of the move by drawing in his paw. The basket tilted a few times, and then settled down.

Gorobei made one more attempt. "Lady Yuri, it's all very well for Zenta to carry Raiko around, but what about yourself? This morning you were too proud to be carried. What will you do this afternoon when the walking gets too rough?"

It was no use. "I can walk anywhere you can walk," Yuri declared. Clearly there was no way to stop her from coming along except by using force. Rolling his eyes heavenward as if to seek help from the gods, Gorobei gave way.

They went around to the back of the mansion, and now they were looking at that half of the island on the side facing the open sea and away from the mainland. For the first time Kajiro fully appreciated the garrison's dominant position. The mansion looked down on the farmhouses and the fishing village, which contained the only harbor and the only approach to the island. Except for the mansion, the only sizable habitation was the convent, which was on the opposite side of the island from the fishing village. Invaders hoping to use the convent for cover would be vulnerable, since they would have to pass in front of the mansion on their way up from the harbor.

Kajiro suddenly realized that he was thinking like a man who had been given the responsibility for defending the island against attackers. He smiled wryly. He was getting ideas above his station. For the present he should apply his wits to the mystery of the missing animals. Perhaps he could also play the role of peacemaker between Yuri and Gorobei. Already they were looking at each other with measuring eyes, like two wrestlers in a ring.

"I don't have to ask if Lady Sada or the commander knows about your intention to join us," Gorobei said, as they began their descent from the mansion.

"I didn't see any point in bothering Sada," Yuri said airily. "She has enough on her mind."

"I should point out that we're going to search the convent first," said Gorobei. "Are you sure you want come along? I know you hate the place."

Again Yuri's lower lip jutted out. "Yes, I do want to come along." She turned to Kajiro. "I've been feeling uneasy about the convent ever since my last visit there. Sada took me to call on the abbess, who is our great-aunt, and the abbess suggested that it would do me good to join the convent. But I don't want to!" Her voice rose a little at the end.

Kajiro heard real panic. "She can't make you join against your will!" he said. He put on a reassuring smile. "Besides, you can't go without Raiko, and they won't take him in the convent since he's a tom!"

Yuri tried to smile back, but the uneasiness remained in her eyes. "Sada says I'm too wild, and she's getting tired of looking after me. And lately my brother-in-law has been saying that he also thinks the convent would be a good idea."

Up to now, Kajiro's impression of Yuri's brother-in-law, the commander, had been a complete blank. This was a good opportunity to learn more about the man. "What sort of person is the commander?" he asked. "Is he really serious about sending you to the convent, even if you hate the idea?"

"You can never tell what my brother-in-law is thinking," muttered Yuri. "Even Sada doesn't know. But I think he really would like to see me put away into the convent."

Kajiro couldn't think of anyone less suited to convent life than Yuri. "Why would he like to see you there?"

Ahead of them they saw the convent behind a fence of bamboo stakes. Rising above the fence were buildings with roofs of dark cypress shingle. The unpainted convent buildings, set on the rocky headland, made a stark picture.

Yuri's eyes were somber. "My brother-in-law would like to put me in the convent because he feels that his own position is insecure. You see, our father was originally the commander on the island, and since he had no son, Sada's husband was adopted to succeed him."

Kajiro had suspected something like this. It explained why Lady Sada was so domineering, since the men of the garrison would be loyal to her and her family, rather than to her husband. "I see," he said. "If he's commander only through marriage, then anyone married to *you* . . ."

Yuri nodded. "Exactly! Some ambitious samurai might marry *me* and make himself a rival to him." As she spoke, she looked at Gorobei and smiled spitefully.

The hint was too obvious to miss. "I don't see why we're wasting our time with idle gossip," said Gorobei stiffly. "Let's get on with the search."

They were almost at the gate of the convent. Here the sea was so close that they could hear waves dashing against the rocks below. Mixed with the pounding of the waves were the shrieks of sea gulls, sounding curiously like women crying in distress.

Kajiro felt the basket heave and tilt in his hand again, as Raiko suddenly shifted his weight. The cat looked bigger, and Kajiro saw that his fur was standing up stiffly. Raiko didn't like the looks of the convent either.

Kajiro gazed at the convent on its bleak promontory. "I would have expected a Shinto shrine here, dedicated some spirit protecting us against the sea," he said thoughtfully. "It's an unexpected place to find a convent."

"My nurse told me there used to be a shrine here," Yuri said. "Its guardian deity protected the island against the ogres."

"I thought you said the stories about ogres were so much local superstition," said Kajiro.

"Of course they are!" said Yuri, with some of her old spirit. People here tell these fairy tales to frighten the children and make them behave."

"What happened to the shrine?" asked Kajiro. "Is it part of the convent now?" It was not unusual for Shinto shrines to be incorporated into Buddhist temples or monasteries.

"There's no trace of the shrine left," said Yuri. "A terrible storm swept it all away, and people decided this wasn't a good place to have a shrine. So they built the convent here instead."

They stood and looked at the swooping sea gulls. Finally Gorobei stirred. "Come on, let's go and announce ourselves to the nuns."

The convent gate opened immediately at their approach, almost as if they had been expected. A black-robed young nun bowed deeply and silently to them. At her gesture, they followed her down a stone-paved path that led across a sandy courtyard. Kajiro had never been inside a convent before, and he was not prepared for the dead quiet of the place. Naturally women who had devoted themselves to religion would not be noisy chatterers, but the extraordinary stillness gave the impression that all life was in a state of suspension.

Kajiro found himself trying to walk on tiptoe. He glanced at his companions, and saw that they were equally subdued. Only Raiko stirred restlessly. Once he moved so suddenly that he nearly spilled out of his basket.

The nun who was conducting them scurried forward in furtive little steps, although she was not particularly short in stature. From the very first, she had her head studiously lowered and did not meet their gaze.

Out of the corners of his eyes Kajiro thought he saw the figures of other nuns. Too shy to expose themselves to the eyes of strangers, they lurked in deep shadows or behind thick wooden pillars. Their presence was revealed only by the fluttering of a black sleeve or a head quickly withdrawn. Kajiro felt like a crass intruder.

They had to call on the abbess before they could start their search of the convent. "I'm terrified of her," whispered Yuri. "That's another reason why I can't stand the thought of living in this place."

Kajiro looked curiously at the girl. "If you can't stand the convent, why did you insist on coming here with us?"

"I want to take this opportunity to tell the abbess once and for all that I don't intend to join the convent," replied Yuri. Then she smiled at him. "It's much easier to do that if I'm with you than if I came with my sister and brother-in-law."

The building they entered contained the living quarters of the nuns. The rooms and corridors looked clean and in good repair, but not a single ornament softened the cheerlessness of the dark woodwork, the beige-colored plastered walls, or the plain white paper in the doors. Kajiro felt chilled, although it was a mild spring day outside.

Most of the doors they passed were closed, but through the shoji, the sliding doors covered with translucent rice paper, they could see here and there dark, motionless shapes. The nuns all seemed to be frozen in place while the intrusion of the searchers lasted.

The abbess was in her study. It was the only room Kajiro had seen so far that contained a few touches of luxury. His eyes were first drawn to a scroll painting hanging in an alcove. The alcove was framed by a pillar made from a natural tree trunk, chosen for its elegant shape. The room, after all, had to accommodate a lady from an aristocratic family.

The abbess wore a white cloth hood covering her shaven head as far as her forehead. From below, the folds of the hood concealed her neck up to her chin, so that only the middle of her face was left uncovered. She was older than Kajiro had expected. From what Yuri had said, he had thought the abbess would be a formidable woman in her prime. Instead, she had the wizened look of the very old. Seated on a flat brocade cushion, she was huddled over as if her sinews had contracted. She was so tiny that the young nun who was conducting the visitors seemed husky and towering.

The abbess might be frail of body, but she was not senile: Her eyes, glittering under her shaven brows, were fully alert. She dismissed the young nun, who retreated and stationed herself by the door. Giving the visitors a brief nod, the abbess fixed her eyes on Yuri. "Well, Yuri, have you come to join our convent?"

The girl raised her head from her deep bow and her lower lip jutted out. "No, Great-Aunt," she said in a clear, firm voice. "I've come to tell you that I will not join the convent—not now, not ever."

Kajiro could tell from the stiff set of Yuri's shoulders that she was braced for reproaches from the abbess. But the old woman only nodded and said, "Very well, if that's the way you feel."

It was an anticlimax. Yuri's shoulders slumped with relief, and her eyes widened at the mild response. For a strange moment Kajiro had the impression that the abbess's shoulders also slumped with relief. If so, the movement was so slight that it was almost imperceptible. He could have been mistaken.

The abbess turned to Gorobei. "Why have you come today? Surely it wasn't just to give moral support to my niece?"

Gorobei's smile was apologetic. "We still haven't found the missing animals, your ladyship. We're doing another thorough search of the island, and that includes the convent grounds. If you have no objections, we will inconvenience you again."

"My objections will be useless in any case," the abbess said tartly. "Now that I've heard Yuri's declaration, there is no point in prolonging the interview. You may commence the search. You must think we're so busy with our prayers that we would miss hearing the cackling of some chickens being hidden on our premises."

As they bowed deeply again and left the room, Kajiro was thinking about the expression he had seen on the abbess's face. Her lips had been curved in sardonic amusement, but her eyes showed a different expression: fear.

Kajiro decided to start their search with the kitchen. "If the missing chickens were brought here, they would most likely wind up on the kitchen chopping board," he said. "After years of vegetarian food, the nuns may have suddenly acquired an uncontrollable craving for chicken meat."

The young nun who was conducting them stopped abruptly. She turned, raised her head, and threw him such a look of outrage that he cringed. "I was just joking!" he protested.

"Well don't let your joke reach the ears of the abbess," Gorobei said dryly. "Otherwise she'll have *your* head on the chopping block."

As they reached the kitchen, they were attacked by a powerful stench. "I don't know what they cook in the convent," muttered Yuri, "but I'm certainly glad I won't be eating here."

They soon saw the cause of the stench. In the middle of the kitchen floor was a broken crock containing radishes pickled in a paste of fermented rice bran. Two of the nuns were on their knees cleaning up.

"Do we have to search the kitchen?" asked Yuri, holding her sleeve over her nose. "There's obviously no room to hide a chicken here, much less a dog."

"We might as well have a look since we're here," said Kajiro, sliding open cupboards and peering inside. He glanced back at the two nuns, who were scooping up the reeking brown paste and yellow radishes. "Strange, isn't it, that pickles can smell so awful and taste so good!"

He could not see anything that seemed out of the ordinary. Being unfamiliar with the workings of a kitchen, however, he was not really a good judge. Nor was Yuri any better. The girl didn't look as if she had stepped inside a kitchen more than twice in her life, if that.

As far as Kajiro could see, he found only utensils that normally belonged in a kitchen: knives, chopping boards, scoops, strainers, and cooking pots of various sizes. The rice bin, a large wooden box lined with tin, was the only container big enough to hide chickens. But it held only rice, and not very much rice. The grains barely covered the bottom of the box.

"These nuns hardly eat enough to stay alive," murmured Kajiro. He was obviously wasting time in the kitchen. Perhaps he felt the need to examine the convent so thoroughly because of the fear he had seen in the abbess's eyes. What could be the cause of it?

Kajiro had seen all he wanted to in the kitchen, but before he could leave, Raiko escaped from his basket. Yuri and Gorobei, assisted by the nuns, made futile snatches at the cat.

Kajiro did not join the hunt, but merely stood watching as the others rushed around. "Why aren't you helping us catch Raiko?" demanded Yuri, glaring at him.

"I'd only get in the way," replied Kajiro. "Besides, the last time I tried to capture Raiko, I got a kick on the shin."

"It's no use," panted Gorobei, stopping to rub his nose. He had crashed into one of the nuns, who was rubbing her shaven head and looking dazed by the encounter.

"I don't know what cats look like when they're laughing," added Gorobei, "but from the way Raiko's whiskers are twitching, I suspect he's having more fun than we are."

Yuri finally remembered that she was carrying a bit of dried squid intended for Raiko's dinner. With that as bait, she was able to tempt the cat from behind the stove and grab him. "You naughty, naughty boy!" she said, thrusting him back into his basket with his tidbit.

"He must have heard a mouse," suggested Gorobei, "and wanted to investigate."

"I wouldn't have thought there'd be enough food here to attract mice," remarked Kajiro, as they left the kitchen and made their way to their next destination.

They were searching the sleeping quarters next, but as soon as Kajiro saw the rooms, he decided that a search would be futile. In the back of his mind had been the thought that one or two of the nuns could be hiding something, some forbidden food they didn't want the rest to know about.

But now he saw that the nuns all slept together in two large connecting rooms. There were no folding screens providing privacy and dividing one person's territory from another's. All he could see were the bare, gleaming, black-bordered tatami mat that covered the floor.

The rooms contained no furnishings. The searchers didn't even see the small cosmetic stands for combs, or wooden hairpins, such as the poorest peasant woman would have possessed. Of course. Since the nuns all had shaven heads, they would have no use for combs or hairpins. None of the women had even a corner of a cupboard for stowing away private possessions. They had no private possessions.

Nevertheless, Kajiro dutifully went through all the cupboards. He was not surprised to find that they contained only bedding. To make their search a thorough one, they shook out every piece of the bedding.

Yuri became increasingly mutinous as they went through the tedious job of taking out each quilt and mattress. "Do we really expect to find chicken bones in the mattresses?" she grumbled.

About a third of the way through, they no longer bothered to refold the bedding, but simply stuffed it back into the cupboards in an untidy heap. All three searchers sighed with relief when they put away the last quilt and slid the cupboard door closed. Yuri sneezed.

Kajiro was suddenly struck by a thought: The cupboards they had left behind them were untidy, but no more untidy than before their search. The bedding they had taken out had not been properly folded in the first place. Never in a private home or in any of the inns he had visited—and he had visited some memorably slovenly inns—was the bedding in the cupboards put away without being folded properly. Here in the convent, the bedding was not only untidy but musty, as if it had not been aired for some time.

The bleakness of the lives led by the nuns suddenly depressed Kajiro. They didn't even have the will to keep their quarters tidy and pleasant. It was a wretched thought. He glanced at Yuri, whose face looked pinched and white. Now that she had faced the abbess and made her declaration, she was obviously anxious to leave.

Kajiro could tell that Gorobei also wanted to be gone. The officer had joined the search with an air of great patience, and had not shirked his part in taking out the bedding. But his politeness did not conceal his evident belief that they would find nothing. He had personally led a search party to the convent once before, after all.

Leaving the sleeping quarters behind them, the search party had to admit that no trace of the missing animals could be seen. Kajiro still felt, however, that something was not quite right about the convent. It would be easy to keep secrets in a place like this, where no one spoke, where the inmates led separate lives despite their physical closeness.

But Kajiro knew little more than he had before the search. What had he learned? Pickled radishes smelled worse than they tasted, and nuns did not take much trouble with the way they folded their bedding. What possible significance could there be in these trivial facts?

Chapter 5

Yuri's jauntiness returned as soon as the convent gate closed behind them. "That wasn't as bad as we thought, was it?" she said to Raiko, whose basket she was now carrying. "Poor baby, you wanted to hunt for mice in that dirty old kitchen, didn't you?"

She continued to babble nonsense. Kajiro guessed it was from relief at leaving the silent convent. He couldn't blame he, for he could feel the relief himself. The place was undeniably oppressive.

Gorobei caught his eye and grinned. "Nauseating, isn't it, that baby talk?" he whispered. "I'm surprised the cat has any appetite left."

Gorobei's voice was not quite soft enough. Yuri heard, and turned furiously. "No more nauseating than the flattery you poured on my sister when you were hoping to marry her!"

Gorobei flushed. "I was not attempting to flatter your sister. I was merely showing proper respect to your family when your father came and took command of the island."

"Respect!" said Yuri. "I noticed that none of the respect reached down to me!"

"Lady Yuri, you were not quite twelve years old when your family arrived five years ago," said Gorobei, recovering his humor. "I couldn't very well treat you the same way I treated your sister, who was already an adult."

As Yuri fumed, Kajiro did some adding and concluded that the girl was nearly seventeen, older than he had guessed. Her behavior was quite immature at times. And yet her analysis of her brother-in-law's motive was startlingly sophisticated. Perhaps her willfulness was simply rebellion against a formidable and domineering older sister. A touch of jealousy might be there as well.

"Well?" asked Gorobei, not quite concealing his impatience. "Shall we continue our tour of the island? It's getting close to dinnertime, and I'm hungry."

Kajiro stood looking at the sea gulls swooping in an aqua sky. He was fascinated by their almost human cries. "I'd like to examine this headland before we go back." Ignoring Gorobei's look of surprise, he walked to the edge of the cliff and peered down at the churning water on the rocks below.

"Look!" exclaimed Yuri. "Is that a whirlpool over there?" She had put down Raiko's basket and was also standing at the edge of the cliff. She pointed at a spot a little distance from the shore.

Kajiro looked, and saw a white, foamy, circular patch. It was definitely a whirlpool. "Has it always been there?" he asked.

Something nagged in the back of his mind. What was it? Was it a remark made by the fisherman that morning in his cottage? "I wonder how far it is from here to the whirlpool," he mused.

"Stop him! Stop him!"

The voice was Yuri's, and the streaking animal was Raiko. For a moment it looked like a repeat of Raiko's previous performances.

"He'll fall over the cliff!" cried Yuri.

Raiko was too canny an animal to fall over. But several times he came to the very edge of the cliff. He led them in an exhausting dance. All we need are some drummers and flute players, and we could have a village festival, though Kajiro, as he made a futile snatch at Raiko's tail.

Once his heart missed a beat when Gorobei's foot slipped and he scrabbled frantically for a handhold on the rocky edge of the cliff to prevent himself from going over.

"This is pointless," panted Kajiro, resigning from the chase. Even if he had learned nothing else, his recent experiences had taught him that human beings could rarely hope to corner a cat. It would be different if he had another fish basket.

"We're just wasting energy," he told his companions. "Look at that cat! He isn't in any danger whatever. He thinks this is a game."

At his words, Yuri, who was pausing to rub a stubbed toe, looked up. After a moment she grinned. "I guess you're right. And this isn't the first time he's done it, either, if we count our chase at the harbor this morning."

"Then that makes it the third time today!"

growled Gorobei. "He'll do it again if we give him a chance."

"Look. Raiko has already stopped running," said Kajiro.

It was true. Now that Raiko was no longer being chased, he sat down and proceeded to lick his paw.

Gorobei sat down heavily on a grassy hump and worked a pebble out of his sandal. "It seems to me that we've spent more time this afternoon chasing that miserable cat than searching for the missing animals. Now if *Raiko* had been the one who was stolen, you could look on me as the chief suspect."

"That's a horrible thing to say!" cried Yuri. "You're the one who knocked over Raiko's basket in the first place! You startled him into running away!"

"I did not!" protested Gorobei.

"Yes, you did!" said Yuri, stamping her foot. "I saw you!"

They sounded like two squabbling children. Kajiro was surprised that Gorobei had descended to Yuri's level. This tendency to quarrel was dangerously contagious, and if he didn't take care, he could catch it himself.

"Do you have any more of the dried squid?" he asked Yuri, as she paused for breath.

Fortunately she did. With another tidbit, she finally succeeded in enticing Raiko back into his basket.

"I hope you've brought a good supply of the

squid," remarked Gorobei. "We may need a lot more of it before we're done."

"Raiko isn't going to run away again," Yuri said stiffly, "as long as you don't kick his basket."

Gorobei had given up trying to deny the charge. He sighed. "All I want to know is this: Just why are we taking the cat along?"

"I can think of one reason," said Kajiro, coming to Raiko's defense. "Cats have a good sense of smell, much better than ours. They can also see better in the dark."

Yuri nodded triumphantly, while Gorobei raised his brows and creased his forehead. They both began to speak at the same time.

"Let's get back for dinner and then continue our search," Kajiro suggested quickly, before a fresh squabble could break out. "Raiko isn't the only one who's hungry. The exercise has given me a good appetite too." He took over the cat's basket again, resolving that on the next leg of his search, his companions would not include either Yuri or Gorobei—or, preferably, both.

He could not help stealing a glance at Yuri. She had put on her straw hat and covered her head, but he could still see a lock of hair that had worked loose. With her cheeks pink from the exercise, she was almost pretty. He liked the graceful way she moved. Her steps had a lightness not often seen in pampered girls who spent much of their time indoors.

He wondered about her abrasive manner toward Gorobei. Why was she always looking for opportunities to insult him? Was it really from dislike? For that matter, Gorobei had contributed his share of comments about Raiko that were needlessly insulting, almost as if he wanted to provoke the girl.

And yet, despite their constant bickering and barbed comments to each other, the officer and the girl had this in common: They were both young people with their futures ahead of them. Kajiro was at most a year older than Gorobei, but he felt a generation removed. He forced himself to remember his position and his condition. He was a penniless ronin weakened from drink, while Gorobei was a handsome young samurai of good standing.

Resolutely turning his eyes away from Yuri, away from Gorobei, Kajiro looked out at the sea. The whirlpool caught his eye again. Suddenly he remembered what it was he had heard at the fisherman's cottage. It was something the old grandfather had said.

"I wonder how far it is from the base of the cliff to the whirlpool?" he murmured.

Gorobei looked at him curiously. "Why do you want to know?"

"I want to know whether something thrown from the cliff can reach the whirlpool," said Kajiro. He stooped and picked up a pebble. Walking to the edge of the cliff directly in front of the whirlpool, he drew back his arm and threw the pebble. He overshot.

"Hmm . . ." he considered. "Of course that pebble was too light." He found a stone the size of a large turnip, and threw it with all his strength. The stone went into the whirlpool and disappeared.

Yuri was quickly losing her patience. "Stop being mysterious! What are you doing?"

Instead of answering, he asked, "Do you think a chicken would weigh more than that stone?"

Yuri stared. He could see that she understood him. "Do you mean that the missing animals were thrown into the whirlpool?" she whispered. "But why?"

"As sacrifice," said Kajiro grimly. "To appease the ogres."

"As sacrifice!" exclaimed Gorobei. "You think the farmers would really throw their own chickens and dogs into the whirlpool?"

"If the farmers are frightened enough," replied Kajiro.

"Yes, it's possible," Gorobei said slowly. "I've felt for some time that something is affecting the people on the island, terrorizing them. In the old days, they even made human sacrifices when times were very hard."

Yuri shook her head furiously. "I don't believe a word of it! You can throw a chicken as far as the whirlpool, but you can't throw a dog that far!"

"Yes you can—one piece at a time," said Kajiro.

Before Yuri could stop him, he undid the catch on Raiko's basket and tipped the cat out. This time, Raiko perversely sat down and calmly washed his face. His face done, he proceeded to groom the rest of his fur, which had been ruffled by his confinement in the basket. Kajiro wanted to nudge the cat into action, but resisted the urge and tried to wait patiently.

Finally Raiko stopped licking. He began to sniff the ground, and soon his sniffing became eager and excited as he got closer to the edge of the cliff. When Yuri reached out to grab Raiko, Kajiro held her back.

Suddenly a low growl came from the cat, and he started to dig at a patch of ground near the edge. Eventually they saw what had excited him. Although attempts had been made to clean the area, Raiko's digging had uncovered some rocks stained with blood. Even more exciting to the cat were slivers of bone.

Yuri's eyes widened with horror. Then she was sick all over her cat.

Once the guest began to mend, his recovery was astonishing. By late afternoon, he was already fretting to be up and about. Sada decided that the best way to keep him in bed was to talk to him and keep his mind occupied.

When she entered the room, the guest was sitting up and eating rice gruel. She noticed that his hand shook a little as he picked up the bowl, but by sheer will he managed to steady it. Perhaps he intended to regain his strength by sheer will as well.

"Yuri and her new friend started the search for the missing animals this afternoon," Sada said. "After combing the convent and the cliffs behind it, the ronin plans to go over to the farmhouses this evening."

The guest looked surprised. "You're letting your sister walk all over the island in the company of a virtual stranger?"

"Of course not," laughed Sada. "They had Raiko, Yuri's cat. Gorobei was also with them, although he hinted that escorting a girl, a ronin, and a cat was beneath his dignity. But I don't think I'll let Yuri out this evening. If the ronin wants to search the farmhouses after dark, he can go alone."

"You're beginning to trust him, aren't you?" asked the guest. "In fact, you think he may actually find something?"

"Yes, it's possible," said Sada thoughtfully. "Drink may have weakened him as a fighter, but he's intelligent. He may notice something that even Gorobei and his men have overlooked. In fact, he said something interesting concerning the missing animals. He thinks the farmers threw them into a whirlpool as sacrifices to the ogres."

"Sacrifices?" said the guest, startled. "The farmers here on the island? Surely they're not as primitive as all that?"

Sada sighed. "We tend to underestimate the

amount of superstition still rampant on our islands. Why, even some of our own men in the garrison are beginning to believe in the ogre stories."

"The sacrifice theory doesn't make sense," said the guest. "The farmers were the ones who first reported the missing chickens. Why would they do that if they themselves had been sacrificing them?"

"I wondered about that, too," admitted Sada. "The ronin suggested that perhaps in the beginning, a couple of chickens were lost through natural causes. Then rumors about ogres were spread—maybe even deliberately—and this caused panic among the farmers. They decided to make sacrifices voluntarily, before the ogres start seizing more valuable animals, or even human beings."

After thinking over Sada's suggestion, the guest shook his head. "That sounds too involved."

He had finished his rice gruel, a good sign. Since the maid had been sent out of the room, Sada herself poured a cup of weak tea and handed it to him. For an instant her fingers touched his, and she could feel her face grow hot.

To cover her confusion, she looked aside and began to speak quickly. She described the search at the convent, and mentioned the scramble to capture Raiko at the cliffs. Introducing some lightness and humor into the sickroom would be beneficial, she thought.

The guest was looking into his teacup. "There are a few things about the visit to the convent that I find interesting," he murmured. Suddenly his hands tightened around the cup. "I wish I had been there! I also want to look at the cliffs and the whirlpool!"

"At the rate you're improving, you'll be able to go yourself in a day or two," said Sada. She used the bracing tone that was supposed to soothe fractious patients.

The guest put down his teacup and leaned back against his brocade-covered armrest. "Do you think you can go over Yuri's account of the search again? I want to make sure I remember all the details."

Patiently, Sada repeated what Yuri had said. This time she described the spilled radish pickles, which she had forgotten to mention earlier. The guest listened with intense concentration—even the most trivial detail seemed to interest him.

"Yuri is observant," he remarked, when Sada finished. He smiled. "I saw her only briefly, but it struck me that she wasn't showing you quite the respect due to an older sister."

Sada smiled back. "Since our parents died, Yuri doesn't show *anyone* much respect. Actually we get along reasonably well. She was feeling less defiant today, probably because she no longer has to go to the convent."

"Yuri does seem to make an unlikely nun," said the guest. He looked at her curiously.

"Whose idea was it to have her enter the convent? Your husband's?"

"Yes," said Sada, not bothering to keep the contempt from her voice. "When he first thought of the plan, he pushed it vigorously, and even convinced the abbess to apply pressure on Yuri. But now he seems to have forgotten about the whole thing."

The guest fell silent. Just as Sada prepared to leave, he spoke about a different matter. "I think we're agreed that the missing animals and the ogre stories are connected with the plot to restore the old lord to power."

Sada nodded. "I'm certain now that the ogre stories are connected with the exile. Whoever is spreading the rumors wants to give the impression that the old lord has supernatural powers."

"What disturbs me," said the guest, "is that we have not had any definite news from the mainland about the rebels, and whether they are having any success in gaining support."

Sada tried not to feel alarm. "There was a storm. Nobody could cross over. That ronin was the last person to reach the island."

The guest looked grave. "The storm is over, and the sea has been calm for most of the day. We still haven't had news. Is it possible that the rebels already control the coastal town on the mainland? If that's the case, I'm afraid we're cut off."

Chapter 6

Dinner was a miserable ordeal. Kajiro ate with Gorobei and several of his men, and the meal started out well enough. His appetite was good after all the walking. Then the serving girl poured wine for him. He drained his cup avidly, almost spilling some wine in his eagerness. Since leaving the mainland he hadn't had a drink, and the first cup after a dry spell was always the one he needed most desperately. His hands trembled slightly when he held out his cup to the serving girl for a refill.

As he raised his cup to drink again, he caught Gorobei's eye on him. Contempt he could have borne—in recent months he had become accustomed to it. But what he saw in the eyes of the young officer was pity. That he could not accept. For the rest of the meal he tried to control his drinking, but the effort left him depressed and tired, and he lost even his appetite for food.

Gorobei entertained the company with an account of his efforts to catch Raiko, but even under the laughter, Kajiro could detect a nervousness among the men. When he mentioned his own theory about sacrificing to the ogres, the diners fell silent, and a pall fell over the company. Kajiro was glad when the meal ended, and he could rise and escape from the tantalizing fumes of the wine.

"What are you planning to do now?" asked Gorobei, as Kajiro walked toward the gate.

"I want to see the farmers," replied Kajiro. "Do you still have orders to keep an eye on me?"

Gorobei grinned. "No, apparently you're free to roam as you please without surveillance from me, which is fortunate, since I'll be fairly busy here. If you need company, there is always Raiko."

"No, I prefer to go alone," said Kajiro quickly. "If I hurry, I can get out before Lady Yuri finds out."

But he was already too late. Waiting at the gate, with a basket in hand, was Yuri. This time Kajiro was determined to be firm. "No, Lady Yuri," he said, before she could open her mouth. "You can't come along."

Yuri tried wheedling. "You can't leave us behind now! Raiko and I were very helpful in searching the convent and the cliffs, weren't we?"

From Gorobei came a snort. Yuri turned on him, "Raiko was the one who found the bones and the bloodstains. They're important clues! You're just peeved because he found something you missed!"

Once again the girl and the young officer were bristling at each other. Kajiro hurried to intervene. "It's not that I don't want you along, Lady Yuri. And you're right about Raiko. His keen nose has been very helpful in the search."

He ignored Gorobei's derisive grin. "But I know your sister would not want you walking around the island after dark."

"I don't care what Sada thinks," muttered Yuri.

"But *I* do," said Kajiro. "Lady Sada was displeased about your trip to the fishermen's village this morning, and I wouldn't want to do anything to anger her again. I'm only here on sufferance, and if she blames me for leading you astray, she would have me expelled at once."

Gorobei spoke up, and his tone was no longer provocative. "Zenta is right. If you insist on accompanying him, you'll just get him into trouble."

As Yuri still looked stubborn, the young officer said, "I'm not going on the search this evening either. It's not proper for you to walk around alone with Zenta at night." He added, "Raiko doesn't count as an attendant."

Yuri finally gave way, although she bridled at Gorobei's last remark. When Kajiro left the front gate of the mansion, he could still hear the girl grumbling softly.

The sky was now fully dark, for this was still early spring, and night came quickly. Children were told to go to bed by their parents before they were sleepy. At the thought of children, Kajiro had to smile. Yuri's behavior made everyone treat her like a child. But she was not a child. She was nearly seventeen, old enough to be married. Again he felt a pang.

The moon was quarter full, and in the open country he could see his way well enough. Soon he reached the cluster of farmhouses.

The official purpose of his visit to the farm village was to test his theory about the sacrifices. If it were true, he could calm the fears of the inhabitants and convince them that there was no need to slaughter their animals. Looking at the shabby houses, he felt a surge of pity for the farmers, who seemed barely able to scratch a living.

But to persuade the farmers, he would have to speak to them, and this proved unexpectedly difficult. The first farmhouse wouldn't even open its door to him. No one answered his repeated calls, although he could hear furtive movements from its occupants just behind the door.

He tried another house. When he again failed to get a response, he lost patience. "I know you're home! If you don't open the door, I'll break it down!"

From inside came the sound of low voices, and something like a fierce argument seemed to break out. Finally Kajiro heard the wooden crossbar being pushed aside. The door slid open and a face appeared. "What do you want? We've already gone to bed!"

Kajiro saw a middle-aged woman, confident and robust in build. Her eyes widened slightly when she saw his two swords, but the sight didn't seem to daunt her. Kajiro had discovered on his travels that among farmers, the men were more easily cowed at the appearance of samurai, while the women were sometimes more defiant.

The farm woman made no effort to hide her annoyance. "Don't you know how late it is? It's past the Hour of the Dog!"

"I'm looking for the animals that you reported missing," said Kajiro. He was struck by her surliness. No household liked to be awakened in the middle of the night, but this was hardly that. The Hour of the Dog was only about an hour after sunset. Granted, it was the spring planting season, but even a farm family that had to rise before dawn shouldn't have to go to bed this early.

At the mention of the missing animals, the woman's face became expressionless and she stared at him for several seconds. "The soldiers from the garrison searched around here already," she said finally. "They didn't find anything. And anyway, what business is it of . . ."

Before she finished speaking, Kajiro could hear a faint rattling noise, and it seemed to be coming from the back of the one-room farmhouse. It sounded like a door carefully sliding open. Someone was leaving by the back way while he stood talking to the woman.

Kajiro moved quickly—but not quickly enough. As he rushed down the narrow passageway between the side of the house and an adjoining shed, he had to squeeze past a rain barrel. He was only in time to see a shadowy figure disappear into a gap between some neighboring farmhouses. To give chase was useless. The local people knew the ins and outs of the village much better than he did.

For a moment he wanted to express his frustration like Raiko. It would relieve his feelings to arch his back and indulge in some hissing and spitting. Why were the farmers so obstructive? They had the most to lose. Why didn't they welcome help, like the fishermen?

Since he couldn't question the farmers, he could at least inspect the poultry cages. Perhaps some weakness in their construction caused the birds to escape and run loose.

In some mountainous central regions of the country, farmers built tall, four-story houses where a family of several generations lived together, with their livestock occupying the ground floor. Here in the coastal villages and islands of the Japan Sea coast, the farmhouses were much smaller, and the animals were housed in separate sheds.

The sheds in this farm village were low, mean structures, for most of the island farmers seemed to keep only some poultry and a watchdog. In only one shed did he see a head of cattle, used as a draft animal. Most of the sheds had only chicken coops and lean-to shelters for the watchdogs. If anyone owned a cat, it would sleep inside the house, but at the ground level of the kitchen. All cats but Raiko, that is. He probably broke the rules and slept in his mistress's room.

As he threaded his way among the farmhouse sheds, testing a coop here and there, Kajiro was still puzzled by the strange behavior of the farmers. Here he was, a suspicious stranger skulking around their chicken coops—chickens that they were losing one by one—and no one had come out to challenge him. Didn't they care if he walked off with a chicken under each arm?

He was ready to give up further examination of the farmhouses, at least for the night. It was now late, and in the light of the quarter moon, he couldn't see well enough to do much good in any case.

The village was very quiet, as if the inhabitants were holding their breath, waiting for him to leave. Since coming to the island, Kajiro felt that his senses were regaining some of their keenness. The reason, of course, was that he had been curbing his drinking.

Now the craving for drink suddenly came back. In this silent village, where all the doors were closed against him, the need for wine gripped him—so fiercely that he found himself taking great, shuddering breaths. He waited, leaning against a corner post of the shed, until the worst of the attack passed and his shivering subsided. As he moved away from the post, a strange sound from a neighboring shed made him freeze.

It was the sound of someone slobbering.

Cautiously, he approached the other shed. He was glad to discover that he could still move lightly and silently. Peering in, he found the interior of the shed almost in complete darkness. There was just enough moonlight for him to see a huddled shape in a far corner. That was where the slobbering came from.

His keen senses, so recently regained, saved his life. Hearing a faint rustle behind him, he ducked, then twisted around to face his attacker. Darkness prevented him from making out the features of the attacker, and he had only an impression of a tall, black figure holding a spear. That was the weapon that had narrowly missed him. Inside the shed, which was now at his back, the slobbering sound had stopped.

Kajiro's sword flashed out. The draw was not as fast as it had been in his prime, but it was respectable, and better than it had been for months. He felt a surge of joy and a return of confidence. The black figure with the spear did not frighten him. He had faced spears before, sometimes half a dozen leveled at once.

He was interested to see that after the initial thrust, the black figure did not immediately attack him again. It was treating him warily. What troubled him more was the thing in the shed behind him. He could hear it shuffling closer.

Slowly, he backed down the narrow passageway, until he was clear of the shed. He risked a quick glance behind him down the main street of the village. Sensing a movement from the black figure, he swerved aside and swept up his sword. The spear thrust missed him again but tore his sleeve. His own riposte was wild. Neither of the combatants had reason to be proud of the exchange.

Kajiro continued to back away. His destination was the narrow passage he had gone through earlier. The tall figure in black followed him step by step, still wary, but not about to let him escape.

As the two emerged from behind the shed, Kajiro saw the face of his opponent briefly in the dim light of the quarter moon. For an instant he went rigid with horror.

The face was something from a child's nightmare. He couldn't see the eyes, for a wild shock of pale hair covered the upper part of the face. But the mouth was visible—a huge mouth stretched in a grotesque grin. No laughter sounded; there was only silence. At each corner of the wide mouth was a fang, much too long and too sharp to be a human tooth.

Again the spear was raised, and the movement broke Kajiro's trance. He turned and ran. This was no time to put his courage to the test. In this unfriendly village, with its unfamiliar twists and turns, he had no hope of winning a fight, or even surviving one.

He reached the passageway, and as he squeezed past the rain barrel, he pushed it over sideways, kicked it violently, and sent it rolling. He looked back once, just in time to see the barrel crash into his pursuer. Without waiting to see more, he gained the opposite end of the passage and was on the road out of the village.

Once or twice he checked, listening for sounds of pursuit. But no one seemed to be coming after him. Soon he had to slow to a walk, for his lungs were out of condition and his heart was pounding painfully.

The running warmed him, but as he slowed down he began to feel cold. Suddenly he was overtaken by a powerful shudder. In addition to the fangs, he remembered something else about the figure in black: the two horns poking out of its wild tangle of hair.

Matsuzo woke with a start. He had felt a gentle touch on his shoulder. He opened his eyes to complete darkness, but immediately realized that his view was being blocked by someone standing in front of him. A voice spoke in his ear, so soft that it was like the tickle of a feather. "Don't be alarmed," it said.

Matsuzo recognized Kimi by the faint perfume of her hair oil. He had finally found an opportunity to read the note she had slipped into his hand and knew that an attempt would be made to rescue him, but the note hadn't said when. The suspense had kept him awake much of the night, but he had finally fallen into a doze. Now he was disoriented, and had no idea what time it was.

He felt the sawing of a knife on the rope binding his arms. As the rope fell away, the blood rushed back agonizingly into his hands and arms. He gritted his teeth and waited for the pain to subside.

Kimi was already creeping toward the door. Trained to work without disturbing an inn full of sleeping guests, she could move soundlessly.

Matsuzo looked around the room. It was just light enough for him to see that three of his captors were sleeping on their beds, while the fourth man lay across the door, his sword close at hand. The fifth man, the one with the close-set eyes, had been absent from the inn for most of the previous evening.

Kimi stepped over the man at the door, and Matsuzo watched without breathing, waiting to see if the vibration on the floor would wake him. He drew breath again only when the girl was safely through the door.

And now it came his turn to move. It was a long, tedious process to struggle up on legs stiff from three days of virtual immobility. His greatest worry was that his stiff knees might crack loudly. By the time he finally stood up, he found himself drenched in sweat.

The door was four paces away—four normal paces. He had to take more than a dozen small steps, each one like trying to step on a nest of pigeon eggs without breaking a single one.

Did he hear a check in the snoring of his sleeping guards? No, they were still sleeping as heavily as ever. That was unusual, wasn't it?

Ten years later, he finally reached the door. The man across the threshold had not moved. For an instant Matsuzo considered taking the sword lying so temptingly on the floor. But as he bent down and reached out, he felt a touch on his arm. Kimi shook her head. Then Matsuzo saw that while the hilt of the sword was lying free, the end of the scabbard was under the sleeve of the sleeping man. Moving it might disturb him.

Once in the hallway, Matsuzo and the girl moved a little more quickly. Kimi stopped when they reached the top of the stairs. By dumb show, she indicated that she should go first, and he should place his feet on the same places where she put hers. He understood. She knew exactly which step squeaked, and where.

Downstairs, they went swiftly to the back of the house, and out by the kitchen door. Free! He was free at last!

Matsuzo looked around at Kimi to thank her. From the look of the sky, it was early morning, at least an hour before sunrise. In the gray, pearly light, the girl's face seemed anxious. He realized this was not the time to stop and savor his freedom. As the girl moved toward a narrow alley, he quickly followed her.

He expected to see Zenta at the other end of the alley—surely the rescue had been arranged by his friend. But there was no sign of Zenta. "Where is my friend?" he whispered to Kimi, as the girl paused to peer out of the alley in both directions.

But Kimi only shook her head. "I'll tell you later," she whispered hurriedly. Seeing that the coast was clear, she led the way cautiously down one of the side streets of the town. As they moved carefully through the town, with Matsuzo following the girl, she stopped frequently to check that they were unobserved. He saw that they were moving inland, away from the shore.

Finally they left the last house of the town behind and found themselves on the open road. Kimi stopped as soon as they came to a place where a bank on the side of the road hid them from view of the town. She leaned against a stone road marker and sighed with obvious relief.

Matsuzo was glad to stop. His legs were still unused to hard exercise, although they were feeling better with every passing minute. "You don't think the men at the inn will come after us?" he asked.

Kimi smiled. "They won't. They're probably still asleep. I mixed some distilled liquor with their wine last night—not enough to be detectable, but enough to make the drink twice as strong as they thought."

That explained why the guards had not awakened, although they were men trained to the extreme of alertness. "I hope you won't get into trouble at the inn when you go back," he said.

"I'm not going back," said Kimi. "I have to go and get help. These conspirators at the inn must be reported."

Matsuzo was puzzled. "Then why didn't we report to the local authorities? Your daimyo must have some competent official governing the town. The port is important to the safety of his domain, after all."

"We can't trust anyone in the town," said Kimi. "We don't know who is part of the conspiracy."

"I see," said Matsuzo slowly. "Is this why Zenta couldn't wait for me in the town? Where is he, by the way?"

"Your friend has gone to the island," Kimi told him. "He went over the morning you were captured."

Matsuzo was stunned. All this time, while he was a prisoner at the inn, he was under the impression that Zenta was somewhere near, making plans to set him free. Instead, his friend had already gone to the island, leaving a maid-servant at the inn to arrange his rescue. Matsuzo felt abandoned, and deeply hurt.

Kimi seemed to read his thoughts. "Your friend was wounded during the fighting at the harbor. He decided that by staying, he would be more of a hindrance than a help."

Matsuzo's resentment was instantly replaced by concern. "He was wounded? How badly?"

"I don't think the wound was too serious," replied Kimi. "Your friend was still able to walk. It was my brother's idea to bring him over to the island. My brother is a boatman, you see."

"Is he back?" asked Matsuzo. "He can tell me how Zenta is."

"I haven't seen my brother since he left," said Kimi, frowning. "He should have returned by now."

In spite of the girl's evident anxiety, Matsuzo saw an attractive rosy glow on her face, and the glow seemed to be getting brighter. He realized that the sun was about to rise. Already the silhouette of the road bank seemed touched with gilt, and the morning was fast advancing as they stood talking.

Matsuzo began to share Kimi's uneasiness. "Maybe the storm delayed your brother's return," he suggested.

"Yes, of course," said Kimi quickly. "I expect to see him any time, now. Our best plan is for him to take you to the island. The garrison there must be warned that there is a plot to restore the old lord to power."

"If Zenta is on the island, he would have told them about the plot already," said Matsuzo.

"I'm not sure your friend knew of the plot when he left," said Kimi. "I overheard the men at the inn talking last night. They stopped when I came in, but I heard enough to know this was what they were planning."

It was more serious than he had thought.

96

Matsuzo was now impatient to reach the island. "We'd better go to the harbor as soon as possible, then, and find your brother."

"I can't go with you to the harbor," said Kimi. "I have to go inland, to the next town, and report this conspiracy."

"If your brother isn't back, maybe I can find another boatman to take me," suggested Matsuzo.

Kimi shook her head. "It's better to wait for my brother than to approach another boatman. We don't know which of them have been bribed by the conspirators."

"But if you're not coming with me to the harbor, how will I recognize your brother?" asked Matsuzo.

"You'll know him because his neck is a little bent to one side," said Kimi. "He's been like that since he was injured as a child."

"A neck injury can be dangerous," said Matsuzo. "He was lucky it didn't paralyze him."

"He was running, and bumped into a samurai in the retinue of the old daimyo," said Kimi, her face stony. "The man picked him up and threw him against a tree. He was lucky he wasn't killed."

That explained why Kimi and her brother were so determined to prevent the conspirators from restoring the old daimyo. Before they separated, they discussed how Matsuzo could reach the boats without being seen by the conspirators. The best way, Kimi suggested, was for him to circle the town and approach the water-front from the north.

Despite the girl's words, Matsuzo found it hard to believe that the conspirators could invade the island in a flotilla of fishing boats. How could they hope to land without being seen by the garrison? Even at night, the islanders would surely have guards posted to watch for any unauthorized landing.

Matsuzo glanced at the girl's slim back as she walked away. She was brave and resourceful. She was also pretty, with attractive, arched eyebrows and delicately shaped lips. Her gesture, as she bent her head to illustrate her brother's crooked neck, was unconsciously coquettish. He hoped that she would be safe and would soon find someone who would believe her story.

After separating from Matsuzo, Kimi walked more quickly, without feeling the need for concealment. Now that she was alone she was less conspicuous, and had a better chance of reaching the next township undetected by the conspirators. But she had forgotten the fifth samurai at the inn, the one who had been away on an errand.

Her shock was great when she rounded a curve in the road and found herself face to face with him.

His surprise was equally great. "Kimi! What are you doing here?"

Kimi thought quickly. "Oh, I'm so glad I

found you! Something strange has happened. I heard a noise downstairs at the inn, and when I went to look, I found that the prisoner had escaped!"

The samurai stared intently at her with his close-set eyes. "What were my men doing?" he demanded.

She did her best to look bewildered. "That's the strangest part! They were all fast asleep!"

He seized her arm with a grip that hurt. "Show me!" he said, as he rushed toward the town, dragging Kimi with him.

Chapter 7

This morning Sada shrank even more than usual from paying her visit to the former daimyo. She should not allow herself to be disturbed by the babbling of a madman, and yet what he had said on the previous day about the ogres was uncanny and unsettling. She did not want to meet his sly, knowing eyes, when she and her men were making no progress in solving the mystery of the missing animals.

The expressions of the guards in front of the exile's door did not promise well. "What has he been doing now?" she asked.

The guards would not look at her. Finally one of them said, "You'd better see for yourself, my lady."

Inside, she found the two maids crouched by the door, looking pale. At her dismissal, they bowed and quickly disappeared.

Sada had expected to find the old lord ranting or looking wild. Instead, he was sitting quietly on a cushion, motionless except for a barely perceptible rocking. Sada had seen her old nurse rock gently like that when she sang or recited old tales.

At Sada's entrance, the exile turned and beamed at her. As always, he replied that his treatment had been satisfactory. The maids had been most attentive, and the food delicious.

"There have been no disturbances in the night, my lord?" asked Sada. She noticed a smugness in his manner which she distrusted.

"No—no disturbances at all," he assured her. "Of course I received another visit from my friends, the ogres. We had a very pleasant chat."

"A pleasant chat, my lord?" said Sada, trying to speak casually. "Did they say anything about the missing animals?"

"Ah, yes, that reminds me," said the exile. "The ogres mentioned that since there are only a couple of watchdogs left on the island, they will need other kinds of red meat soon."

"P-Perhaps we can order some from the m-mainland," stammered Sada. "They prefer dogs to other kinds of meat?"

The old lord considered. "They didn't insist on dog. Actually, they enjoy tender human flesh even more, although they will eat other kinds of meat too. Cats, for instance."

"I'll see to it right away," said Sada, her gorge rising. Her exit from the room was more hasty than respectful.

Outside Sada found the guards talking excitedly with the two maids. They fell silent when they saw her.

"What are you whispering about?" demanded Sada.

"Oh, my lady," said one of the maids, the talkative one, "the ronin who went to search the farmhouses last night reported that he saw an ogre! It attacked him and tried to kill him!"

Shocked, Sada refused to believe the report at first. Then she became furiously angry. So! The man had turned out to be an agent of the enemy after all! He had been sent in order to spread panic among the soldiers of the garrison. And she had thought that he was harmless, even helpful. She had made an error in judgment, and she hated to be proven wrong.

"Tell one of the guards to send the ronin to the inner courtyard!" she ordered. "I wish to question him immediately!"

On her way to the inner courtyard, she passed her husband's study. He stepped out from the little room, still holding a writing brush in his hand. A piece of paper with an unfinished poem lay on the low table in the study.

"What is happening, Sada?" he asked. "What are you angry about?"

In a few curt sentences Sada told him about the ronin's claim to having seen an ogre. "If he turns out to be working for the conspirators, I'll have his head!" she muttered.

Her husband noticed that his brush was dripping ink. Hurriedly cupping his hand under the brush, he said mildly, "Can't you wait until after breakfast before questioning him? It's still early."

Sada didn't even bother to answer him. She turned with a crisp rustle of her kimono skirt and swept toward the inner courtyard. Her husband put down his brush and followed her more slowly.

One of the serving women hurriedly placed flat cushions on the wooden veranda overlooking the courtyard. Sada and her husband had hardly seated themselves on the cushions when she heard a step behind her.

Her guest had left his sickroom and was approaching, walking slowly but steadily. "May I watch while you question the man?" he asked.

Sada half rose in alarm. "Should you be up? The morning air is damp, and it's drafty here."

He smiled. "I'm used to damper and draftier air than this. At the moment my worst problem is boredom, from inactivity."

At Sada's command, the maid brought another cushion and a warm padded robe, which the guest was not too proud to accept.

They heard a crunching of gravel, and through a side door the ronin appeared in the courtyard, flanked by two soldiers. The three men bowed down to the ground and waited.

Sada allowed the silence to stretch. When at last she spoke, her voice was icy. "You have been spreading irresponsible rumors about ogres. Is this an attempt to undermine the morale of the garrison?"

The ronin raised his head. He looked composed. "I wasn't intending to undermine morale. Some of your soldiers wanted to know how I got this long slash in my sleeve, and I was telling them what happened to me in the farm village."

Sada's anger changed to confusion. Now that she had seen him face to face again, she found it hard to believe that he was a cunning agent sent by the conspirators. His features were somewhat blurred, but they contained signs of breeding. His eyes were steady and honest. She was beginning to think that her first impression had been correct after all. He was a samurai who had seen better days, who was weakened by drink, but still honorable. Sada turned to her guest to see his reaction.

The guest was studying the ronin narrowly. "Tell us exactly what happened to you in the village."

The ronin spoke slowly, obviously choosing his words carefully. "I wanted to question the farmers about their missing animals. None of them would talk to me, and they all closed their doors in my face. While I was looking around the animal sheds, someone attacked me with a spear. That was how I got this slash."

He paused, and then added apologetically, "What I told your men was true. My attacker had two exceptionally long dogteeth, almost like fangs. He also had two horns on top of his head."

Sada sighed. She couldn't deny that the man talked calmly and sounded sincere.

"I shouldn't have mentioned the fangs and the horns," admitted the ronin. "I had no idea that it would be so upsetting here. The villagers are easily frightened by talk of the ogres, but I thought the soldiers at the mansion would only be amused."

He had framed his words as an apology, but clearly a question was implied. He must have noticed how nervous the garrison became at any mention of the ogres, and was probably wondering why a casual word about horns had brought her wrath down on his head.

Sada turned to her husband and her guest. "Well? What do you think? Shall we tell him about the rumors we heard regarding the plot to restore the exile?"

Her husband had been toying with his fan, opening it half way, and then shutting it. Sada found herself irritated by the snapping sound of his fan. She wondered, not for the first time, whether her husband's blank face hid a profound mind or a perfect vacuum. Just as she was about to turn away impatiently, he finally answered. "Why don't we tell him? There's so much talk here that he'll find out sooner or later, anyway."

Her guest nodded agreement. "He strikes me as a man of sense. I don't think he was exaggerating about his experiences in the farm village. In fact I think that far from making things up, he may have seen something else, something he hasn't mentioned."

"I don't deny his bravery," said Sada slowly.

"And I agree with you about his intelligence," said the guest.

"I don't understand why the farmers should refuse to talk to him," said Sada. "They were the first ones to report the animals missing."

"Something must have happened to change their attitude," said the guest. "Although I still don't accept the theory about the sacrifices. It seems too farfetched."

While Lady Sada, the commander, and the guest were conferring up on the veranda, Kajiro covertly studied them. He could see that Lady Sada had been shaken by his story of the horned and fanged creature. The commander, aside from a brief remark, resumed what seemed to be his normal occupation: staring into space.

Kajiro was most interested in the reaction of the man who was seated off to one side on the veranda. He was Lady Sada's guest, Kajiro had learned, a friend of her family. But the men of the garrison had seen very little of him because he had fallen ill as soon as he arrived. Only now was he well enough to be up. Although he still looked pale, his eyes were very sharp. Lady Sada's demeanor showed that he was someone whose opinion she valued highly.

On the veranda, the discussion was finished and Lady Sada turned again to Kajiro. "I know you are wondering why our men are so unusually edgy, and why we have such a large garrison for such a small island. As you may have heard, we are guarding an important prisoner, the former daimyo of the province, who has been deposed and exiled here after his son assumed power."

Kajiro finally understood the need for extreme security. It was not at all surprising that he had been arrested for landing on the island without authority. "I can see why you need your precautions," he said. "You have heard rumors, haven't you, that there is a move to rescue the former daimyo?"

Lady Sada and the guest exchanged glances. She turned back to Kajiro and nodded. "The old lord still has many supporters in the province."

"But surely you are safe enough?" asked Kajiro. "The island has only the one harbor, and that is constantly patrolled, as I discovered myself."

"There have been certain developments," Lady Sada said carefully.

Kajiro began to understand. "You mean the missing animals, and the stories about ogres?"

Again Lady Sada exchanged a glance with her guest "The exile, the old lord, claims to have supernatural powers," she said. "He says the ogres are his allies, and they have come to help him."

"I see," said Kajiro slowly. From now on he would have to be careful about mentioning fangs.

The guest broke his silence. "I should like to hear more about your search of the convent yesterday."

"The convent!" exclaimed Lady Sada. "How can there be anything suspicious there? My great-aunt has been the abbess at the convent for nearly thirty years! She doesn't permit the slightest irregularity. That's why Yuri hates the place."

"Nevertheless, I'd like to hear about the convent," said the guest. He smiled apologetically to his hostess before turning back to Kajiro. "Tell us about your visit there, and don't omit anything, even if it seems irrelevant."

Kajiro tried to describe every stage of the search. The guest seemed most interested in Raiko's escape from his basket. "So you think the cat smelled something in the kitchen that you didn't?"

"All I could smell were the pickled radishes," said Kajiro, his nose twitching even at the memory. "A crock of pickles was broken, and two of the nuns were trying to clean up while we were there. But I've heard that cats can pick up several scents at once, whereas human noses detect only the strongest one."

At Kajiro's last remark, the guest looked very thoughtful. He seemed to be the only person interested in Raiko, other than Kajiro himself. "Now about the cliffs," he prompted. "You say that it was the cat who discovered the bloodstains?"

After Kajiro finished describing the scene on the cliffs, the guest sat silently thinking for several minutes. He seemed to have an unusual capacity for stillness, an ability to conserve his strength and not waste it on fruitless fidgeting. Finally he looked up. "Was the cat with you when you met the horned figure?"

"No, I was alone at the farm village," said Kajiro. Suddenly he remembered the slobbering thing in the dark shed. The guest had said that he should omit nothing. "I should have mentioned this earlier," he said slowly. "I didn't, because it sounds just as incredible as the figure with fangs and horns."

He had everyone's attention now. Even the commander had stopped staring into space. "Well?" demanded Lady Sada. "What else did you see?"

Kajiro swallowed. "It wasn't so much what I saw—the night was quite dark, after all. It was what I heard: someone in one of the sheds was eating, eating rather noisily."

A loud laugh rang out. It came from the commander. "So! Our farmers don't have very dainty table manners! This isn't exactly startling news!"

Even Lady Sada chuckled, although she couldn't hide a hint of uneasiness. But the guest did not smile. He turned to his hostess. "I'd like to pay a visit to the convent, and to the cliffs as well. Do you think that Raiko the cat would be willing to go there once more?"

Lady Sada sent an attendant for Yuri. The maid returned and reported that the girl had gone out. Apparently Raiko had escaped, and his mistress had gone out searching for him. Since this was a regular occurrence, the maid hadn't thought it necessary to report it. According to the guards at the gate, she had been seen going in the direction of the fishing village.

Lady Sada next sent for Gorobei. When Kajiro left the courtyard, he could hear her angrily questioning the young officer. Gorobei's replies, while spoken in a lower voice, sounded almost as angry.

Kajiro had only one thought. He had to find Yuri and Raiko at once. Animals running loose were not safe on this island, and if anything should happen to her pet, Yuri's grief might lead her into doing something desperate. The men of the garrison, with an important prisoner to guard, might not be willing to spare the time to hunt for a lost cat. This was a job for him, an unemployed ronin.

No one would object if he left, thought Kajiro, or even notice that he was gone. But he was wrong. A soldier caught up with him just as he reached the front gate. The man had an unexpected message: The commander wanted to see him.

Astonished, Kajiro followed the soldier to a small room that looked like a study. The summons reminded him of his mission. This was a good opportunity to study the commander and find out what sort of man he really was. Since coming to the island, Kajiro had become much too absorbed with missing animals, legends about ogres, and most of all, Yuri and her cat.

After dismissing the messenger, the commander did not speak to Kajiro at once. He moved various small objects on his desk, an ink stick, a brush, a water jar. Kajiro tried to contain his curiosity and his impatience as he waited.

Finally the commander cleared his throat. "I've noticed that you displayed some concern and regard for my sister-in-law, Yuri."

The blood rushed to Kajiro's face in a hot tide. The commander, who appeared at first to be a dreamer, was more observant than he had thought. Kajiro himself had not realized the depth of his feelings for Yuri until it was pointed out. He could only stammer in his confusion, "I . . . I . . ."

"Yuri is a difficult girl," the commander continued, as if he hadn't noticed the interruption. "Her sister can do nothing with her. We had thought about sending her to the convent at first—it was an idea proposed by the abbess—but she vehemently refused to go."

Kajiro found his voice at last. "Lady Yuri said that convent life would not suit her."

The commander nodded. His face was smooth and without expression. It was impossible to guess what his feelings really were. "Yuri will soon be seventeen, too old to be running all over the island with her cat."

The picture of Yuri running all over the island with her cat was one he found particularly attractive, Kajiro thought sadly.

Meanwhile, the commander was saying, "As a marriageable young woman, she becomes a target for many ambitious young samurai here—like Gorobei, for instance."

Suddenly the commander looked intently at Kajiro. For once his eyes were not at all dreamy. "I would much rather see her married to someone disinterested, someone who really cares for her."

Speechlessly, Kajiro stared at him.

"You may go," said the commander. Without looking up again, he poured water on the ink slab, picked up his ink stick, and began to grind.

Kajiro left the study with his emotions in a whirl. The motives of the commander, that opaque man, were difficult to read. But one thing was clear: He was jealous of Gorobei. Kajiro was reminded of something Yuri had said earlier. The commander's status was not secure, since he was an adopted son and had been appointed to his position only by marrying Sada, his predecessor's daughter. Perhaps he thought that his position would be jeopardized if the other daughter, Yuri, were to marry an ambitious young samurai like Gorobei. Yuri, however, would pose less of a threat if she were to be married off to a penniless ronin without Gorobei's powerful family connections—someone like Kajiro.

Yuri had taunted Gorobei for having courted Lady Sada unsuccessfully. But Lady Sada's marriage, according to custom, had been arranged by her parents. What if she really preferred Gorobei to the husband chosen for her? The commander would have another reason to be jealous of Gorobei.

A complicated man, the commander. But Kajiro found himself warming to him, and he was ashamed at having been sent to spy on him.

Kajiro left the mansion with his thoughts confused. How did he feel about Yuri? Equally important, how did *she* feel about *him*? About Gorobei?

But first, he had to find her.

Remembering Kimi's advice, Matsuzo avoided the road leading directly back into town. He struck out in a northerly direction at first, clambering over some low hills that followed the contours of the coastline. At one point he thought he was lost, but he was able to recover his bearings, and soon he was relieved to see the sea again. Descent to the shore was difficult, since the ground was rocky, but he relished the exercise. Already he felt a general improvement in his muscle tone. All he needed now was a sword. The fresh air and exercise had given him a sharp appetite, and he quickened his steps.

After reaching the shore, he saw that he was only a short distance north of the coastal town. He could see the first of the houses. Now he had to move more cautiously. Avoid the townspeople, Kimi had said. Avoid all officials. Approach only her brother, the boatman.

That was easy enough to say. How was he to mingle with the fishermen and peer at each one, to see who had a crooked neck? He would be conspicuous. Matsuzo knew that he would always look exactly what he was: a young samurai of good family and polished manners. His attempts at disguises in the past had never been anything but ludicrous.

Nevertheless, mingling with the fishermen was what he had to do. He couldn't skulk behind a tree or a house and spy on them. That would look even more suspicious.

He straightened his clothes and brushed off some dirt that came from his climbing. Assuming a nonchalant air, he stepped down to the beach, where some dozen or so fishermen were preparing their nets and floats.

One of the men was working to free a strip of dried kelp tangled in his net. Surely his neck was a little crooked?

Matsuzo sauntered up to him and cleared his throat. "Ahem. Annoying, aren't they, these little bits of seaweed?"

The man glanced up and stared. His neck now looked perfectly normal.

"Er . . . I'll let you get on with your work," said Matsuzo, retreating quickly.

Next time he would look more carefully before making an approach. His attention was caught by a man scraping barnacles from the bottom of his boat. Now, that man definitely had a crooked neck. Matsuzo sidled over to him, trying not to appear hurried. "Good morning," he said in a bright voice. "Fine day for fishing, isn't it?" The words sounded fatuous as soon as they left his mouth.

The man finished scraping off one last barnacle before looking around. At the sight of the young samurai, he stood up. As his back straightened, so did his neck. Another mistake.

"Ah, to be in the fresh air!" cried Matsuzo, backing away. "How I wish I were a fisherman like you!" He knew that on top of silliness, he was adding an impression of downright lunacy. But he was beyond caring.

The trouble was that unless he had all the fishermen lined up and standing at attention, he couldn't tell which of them had a crooked neck. While a man was at work, his neck was almost always slightly bent to one side.

How about that man, the one who looked rather surly? No, he was normal too. As Matsuzo started to walk off, he heard a step behind him. It was the surly-looking man.

"I can't take you over tonight," the man said to him in a hoarse whisper. "I haven't been bringing in fish at all, and unless I get in a good catch soon, people will be suspicious." With that, he turned away and began to stow his gear busily.

Slowly, Matsuzo walked up from the beach and sat down on a rock a short distance away. He needed time to think. Had Kimi been mistaken? Was it this man who took Zenta across, not her brother? But the man sounded as if he had been expecting Matsuzo to ask him for the ferrying, and for this very evening. It was bewildering.

Then he thought of another explanation. Kimi had mentioned her suspicion that some of the fishermen had been bribed by the conspirators to take them to the island. That was it. This man was one of the bribed fishermen, and he had mistaken Matsuzo for a conspirator.

He heard a faint sound behind him. Whirling around, he saw a fisherman a short distance away, standing and considering him thoughtfully—with his head slightly bent. The man slowly approached, and Matsuzo waited to see if the man's neck would straighten. It didn't. It remained rigidly bent at the same angle.

"You were looking for me, weren't you?" asked Kimi's brother. "I rowed your friend across to the island, and he asked me to do the same for you. I'm sorry I couldn't meet you earlier. The storm delayed me, and after I got back, I had to keep out of sight for quite a while. Well, are you ready to leave?"

Matsuzo needed no urging. As they hurried to the boat, which was beached somewhat apart from the others, the fisherman asked, "What's happened to Kimi? I haven't seen her this morning."

Kimi was trying to hide her fear. Her captor was still holding her arm, and his grip didn't loosen, only tightened. Soon she would have an ugly bruise on that arm. She would be lucky if that was all she would receive. It was no use trying to talk to her captor again. His only response had been a grim silence as he hurried her along. She wondered dully if the men at the inn had awakened yet.

Well before they reached the inn, it was obvious that the men were awake. From the street outside they could already hear angry male voices, the sound of slaps, and a woman's shriek. Up the street a few doors were sliding open and heads were cautiously poking out.

"The stupid fools!" snarled Kimi's captor, pulling her after him into the inn. His temper was not improved by the sight that greeted him.

His four men, looking disheveled and panicked, were in a downstairs room of the inn. One of them was holding a maidservant by the hair. On both of her cheeks were angry red marks.

"Just what do you think you're doing?" the new arrival demanded. "I could hear you all the way down the street!"

The four samurai stared at their leader in dismay. The man who was holding the maid released her, and she sank moaning to the floor.

"Well?" said the leader.

The men shuffled their feet. Finally one of them spoke up. "Somebody at the inn released the prisoner. When we woke up, he was gone. His rope was cut."

"And what were you doing while his rope was being cut?" asked the leader icily.

117

The four men could not meet his eyes. "They must have put something in our food," said the man who had struck the maid. "That's why we all overslept."

"Oh yes?" said the leader. "One of those tasteless and odorless drugs that we read about in storybooks?"

A second man suddenly pointed at Kimi. "She did it! She's the one who always serves our food!"

Slowly the leader turned and studied Kimi. His close-set eyes darkened with suspicion.

The door of the inn opened, and standing outside was a file of soldiers. "We have a report of some disturbance here," announced the man at their head. "My officer wants to know what is happening."

The leader of the conspirators smiled. "Ah, yes. I was just planning to have a word with your officer. I have some orders for him."

Chapter 8

Yuri was not ready to lose hope, but she could not control her mounting anxiety. The people at the island's small fishing village had been kind, and some of them, especially the children, had helped her look for Raiko. Cries of "Here, kitty, kitty," produced no result, however. Nor did strips of dried squid, dangled enticingly in front of every dark corner where the cat could be lurking. If Raiko did not emerge for his favorite food, he was definitely not at the fishing village.

Her next stop was the cliffs behind the convent. Raiko had been excited by the bits of bone and bloodstains he had discovered there. Perhaps he was digging there in the hopes of finding more.

She was reminded of what Zenta had said about sacrifices. Should she go back to the mansion and get his help? When she first discovered that Raiko was missing, she had hoped that he would join her in looking for the cat. But it seemed that he had been summoned to an audience with her sister, and there was no telling how long the session would last. Yuri didn't want to wait. She felt a sense of urgency, a belief that she had no time to lose. Chickens and dogs might be sacrificed by the islanders, but not her cat, not Raiko. He was too clever to be

caught by superstitious peasants. Although—
she stifled a sob—even the cleverest animal
could be trapped if the bait were tempting
enough.

She was even more frightened by the story
of the horned creature that had attacked Zenta.
He had tried to make light of the incident, admit-
ting that it had been too dark to see properly.
But Yuri believed him. He was not the kind of
person who made up stories.

Why was she so ready to trust him? Sada had
mentioned his name once, and Yuri had pic-
tured a conceited young samurai, someone like
Gorobei, perhaps. That young officer thought
every girl on the island would become his slave
just because he was handsome and had good
family connections. But Zenta was different.
Yuri had been astonished to find him gentle,
almost humble. She blushed a little when she
recalled how ungrateful she had been, how she
had kicked him when he was trying to catch
Raiko for her on the beach. But instead of
reproaching her, he had been understanding
and kind. At the thought of Raiko, however, her
anguish returned and her eyes filled with tears.

A strong wind was blowing at the top of the
cliffs, and Yuri had difficulty even keeping her
feet. She found the patch of ground where Raiko
had been digging. Sand had blown over the area,
but could not quite hide the bloodstains on the
rocks. There was no sign of her cat. Yuri called
and called. It was as if the wind blew her voice

right back into her throat. She raised her voice higher, almost to a shriek, for she remembered that Raiko's ears were acute at picking up higher sounds. But she heard no response.

Her throat became raw with shouting, and she finally admitted that Raiko was not going to appear. As she turned away, a thin wail made her heart stop. Another wail. And then she remembered that she had heard this sound before: It was the crying of sea gulls. There was a variety of gulls called "cat gulls," because their cries sounded exactly like those of a cat. Yuri turned away quickly for she could not bear to listen to these cries, which reminded her so much of Raiko.

She had only one more place to search, the convent. The temptation was even greater now to go back and ask for Zenta's company. But that would take too long. Slowly, she walked to the gate of the convent, the place she hated.

The gate opened at once, and she knew that she had been seen from a distance.

The young nun who opened the gate was the same one who had conducted the search party on the previous day. As before, she kept her face lowered. "Yes?" she asked in a hoarse whisper.

"I'm . . . I'm looking for my cat," quavered Yuri. "I think he may have wandered in here by mistake."

The nun bowed silently, and as she straightened, Yuri caught a glimpse of her face. She was smiling broadly, and showing two rows of strong white teeth.

Yuri's instinct shouted at her to turn around and escape before it was too late, but her fears for Raiko prevented her. Mastering her revulsion, she followed her guide across the courtyard of the convent.

On the previous day, the courtyard had been nearly deserted, and the only nuns she saw had been standing half hidden in the shadows or behind pillars. Today she was aware of a great many more of the black-robed figures. As she walked past, some of the black figures stepped forward and turned until they were fully facing her. They were all smiling.

To her surprise, Yuri was not conducted to the abbess. When she questioned her guide, she was told curtly that the abbess was resting and could not be disturbed. Stung by the insolent manner of the reply, Yuri drew herself up. "Do you know who I am? The abbess is my great-aunt!"

The nun stopped, turned, and again showed her white teeth. "But of course. You are Lady Yuri, the sister-in-law of the island's commander. And you have come to look for your poor, lost kitty."

The room they finally entered was a reading hall for Buddhist scriptures, and on the polished wooden floors were rows of round straw cushions. Only one was occupied: A black-robed nun with a white hood was seated on it cross-legged. Yuri saw a face with heavy, coarse features, a face without a trace of pity.

Yuri's legs trembled as she sat down. She had never been so frightened in her life. Suddenly she remembered something her sister had told her. "Proving that you're braver than the boys doesn't mean that you have to run faster or climb higher than they do, Yuri," Sada had said. "Adults prove their courage in a different way."

Yuri forced herself to gaze steadily at the ruthless face of the seated nun. She took a deep breath, and was glad when she spoke to find her voice steady. "I'm sorry to disturb your devotions. The fact is, my cat has run away, and I suspect he may have got into your kitchen again. He was very interested in searching the place yesterday."

The seated nun nodded but did not reply. Her eyes looked amused.

"I'll just have a quick look in the kitchen," Yuri said briskly. "And then I'll be on my way."

The nun broke her silence. "I'm sorry, Lady Yuri, but you are mistaken."

"What?" said Yuri, startled by the resonant timbre of the nun's voice. "You mean you're not going to let me search the kitchen?"

The nun was smiling as broadly as all the others. "I mean that you will not be on your way."

The fishing village reported that Yuri had been there earlier, but had already left. Next Kajiro tried the farming village. Here he found the farmers just as uncooperative as they had been on the night before. No, they had not seen the girl or her cat. No, they would not help him look for them. They were too busy with the spring planting. Since it was undeniably true that this was the planting season, there was little Kajiro could do. Interfering with crop production on this small island, where food was scarce, would not make him popular with Lady Sada or the commander.

He could at least look again into the animal shelters, particularly the shed where he had heard the disgusting, slobbering sound. Things looked different now that it was daylight, and it took him a while to find the right shed At least if anyone attacked him with a spear, he could have a good look to see if the fangs and the horns had been merely his imagination or a trick of the moonlight.

But no horned spearman tried to attack him. Nor was there any sign of Yuri or Raiko. Almost reluctantly, afraid of what he would find, he bent down and examined the ground of the shed for bloodstains or bits of bone. Without the help of Raiko's keen nose, the results of his examination were inconclusive. He saw some dark stains here and there, but they could be animal feed or droppings.

Discouraged, he abandoned the farm village and decided to try the cliffs once again. Raiko had been interested in the area. It would be the logical place for the cat to go. Perhaps he had made a mistake in spending so much time in the farm village. He should have tried the cliffs first.

But when he reached the cliffs, he saw no sign of the girl or the cat. His examination of the ground revealed neither footprint nor pawprint. There wouldn't be, for the strong wind would have blown away any traces in the sandy soil. The wind and the dashing waves also made it difficult to hear, and the only sounds were the shrill cries of the gulls.

Wait—did he hear something new, something he hadn't heard on his earlier visits? He cupped his ears and listened intently.

There was no mistake. On top of the distant shrieking of the gulls, he heard a thin, mewing sound. It seemed to be coming from somewhere close by. His hopes rose, and he looked around wildly. Which direction were the mews coming from?

The sound seemed to grow stronger, and it seemed to be cries of anger rather than of pain. That made him more hopeful yet. Following the direction of the sound, he walked along the edge of the cliff until he came to a group of pine trees. The trees were stunted and leaned back at a sharp angle from the edge, a result of the constant battering from the sea winds.

Kajiro came to an abrupt halt. Someone was standing by the trees and looking down the cliff. Approaching cautiously, Kajiro could hear the man muttering angrily, ". . . confounded animal! . . . drowned him!"

Raiko! He must mean Raiko!

The watcher sensed Kajiro's approach. He whirled about and whipped out his sword. Without uttering a challenge, without asking a question, he lunged out viciously.

But Kajiro's own sword was already in his hands. He ducked under the other man's attack and swept up his sword in riposte, catching his opponent full across the chest. Any sound made by the clash was scattered by the winds.

Panting, Kajiro looked down at his motionless opponent. The exchange had happened so quickly that it was over before he had time to realize what had happened. The other man was a competent enough swordsman, but he had been taken off guard. Still, Kajiro's own performance had been creditable. It looked as if since he came to the island, his reflexes were returning to him little by little.

But his self-congratulation was interrupted by a mew, an angry, impatient mew. He peered over the cliff. On this side of the island, the cliffs were so sheer that they went almost straight down. But here and there, the face of the cliff was broken by small, twisted trees whose hungry roots clung to almost invisible crevasses. In addition, an occasional narrow ledge was carved out by rock fall or erosion from the sea. On one such ledge, no wider than a hand, sat Raiko. He was looking up at Kajiro, and the expression in his squinting eyes said, "What kept you?"

So great was his relief that Kajiro found himself crooning baby talk, almost as nauseating as Yuri's. Another impatient mew from Raiko reminded him that crooning was not as welcome as a good meal to a cold, hungry cat. How Raiko had got to the ledge would have to wait. The problem was how to get the cat off the ledge.

Kajiro lay on his stomach at the edge of the cliff and reached out. But even with his arm stretched full out, his hands were more than eight feet away from the cat.

A small tree, growing not too far from the ledge, gave him an idea. Its base was within his reach, and when he pushed at it with the scabbard of his sword, the tip of one branch came to rest on Raiko's ledge. Now, if Raiko could be induced to climb on that branch . . . "Here, kitty," coaxed Kajiro. "Come on, up you go!"

Raiko looked up, and his expression said, "You can't be serious!"

When Kajiro pushed the tree down farther, Raiko backed away hastily, and began to slide off the ledge. Only by scrabbling frantically did he manage to get back to safety. When he eventually looked up again, he mewed reproachfully.

Discouraged, Kajiro rose, stepped back from the edge of the cliff, and looked around for something that might help him. He turned his eyes away quickly from his late opponent, who still lay motionless on the ground. Then he caught sight of something lying by the clump of pine trees. There, almost as if the gods had answered his prayer, lay a coil of rope. One end of the rope was even helpfully tied around the trunk of a tree.

Half expecting the rope to vanish at his touch, Kajiro cautiously tested its thickness and the tightness of the knot. Both were perfect. Why refuse a gift when it's offered? Tying the loose end of the rope securely around his waist, he lowered himself over the cliff and began to climb down toward Raiko's ledge. He had put on his cloth mittens, which protected his palms while leaving his fingers exposed and free.

It was difficult to twist his head and look down—in any case, he was more comfortable not looking down at the rocks and foaming waves. But he couldn't tell how much progress he was making. He knew he had reached the cat only when a sharp pain stabbed into his calf. Raiko was digging his claws into his leg.

"All right, Raiko," muttered Kajiro. "Hang on, and don't let go."

Raiko did not let go. Instead, he began to climb. Kajiro winced as he felt the sharp pricks of Raiko's claws ascending his spine. He nearly cried out when the cat reached his shoulders and then clung to the back of his head. At least Raiko didn't scratch his face.

Kajiro did not enjoy the climb back up the cliff with a frightened, overweight cat clinging to his scalp. His face was streaming by the time he reached the final part of the climb. When he at last reached the top of the cliff, his eyes were blurred with sweat.

Which was why he didn't believe what he was seeing: Inches away from his nose was a hideous face with a red, grinning mouth. Blood dripped out of the rigid gaping mouth, and a bloody hand with a knife began to saw on his rope, his lifeline.

Suddenly Raiko's claws tightened for an instant on Kajiro's head, and then the cat launched himself into the air, straight at the hideous head. The face with the red, grinning mouth disappeared from view.

Losing no time, Kajiro flipped himself over the edge of the cliff and landed at last on safe ground. He rolled and was up again in an instant, with his sword out. But he lowered it again when he saw that it was no longer needed.

Raiko, with his back arched and his fur standing up, was hissing at a figure stretched out on the ground. Kajiro recognized his recent opponent, whom he thought he had killed. The man was now truly dead. His eyes were blank and open, and the blood had trickled to a stop from the gaping mouth.

Earlier, Kajiro had not had time to wonder about his attacker's presence. He had been too busy defending himself and then climbing down after Raiko. But now he began to think.

The dead man was a total stranger, Kajiro was certain. He had not seen him among the men of the garrison. What was the stranger doing here, standing guard over a coil of rope? Another question was why the man had attacked him without warning, without even challenging him and demanding to know his business.

Kajiro's conclusion was that the dead man must have been engaged in some clandestine activity, which he wanted to keep secret from the garrison. Kajiro could guess what the stranger's secret was. He was involved with the plot to restore the former daimyo.

A bump against his leg reminded him that Raiko was hungry. The cat was rubbing against him—possibly for warmth. But Kajiro preferred to interpret Raiko's crowding as friendliness. He took out the little packet of dried squid, which had lately become a normal part of his equipment. Raiko fell on the food so hungrily that he nearly gagged.

While the cat was eating, Kajiro's eyes went back to the coil of rope. When he had been using it to rescue Raiko, he had noticed that the rope was much longer than needed—long enough to reach the base of the cliffs, in fact.

Who would want to make this terrifying, dangerous descent down the cliffs? Why not go to the fishing village, where there was a good harbor? The answer, of course, was that the harbor was patrolled.

Raiko was finished, and when a few plaintive mews failed to produce more food, he went exploring at the edge of the cliff. More bloodstains and bones? But the cat wasn't trying to dig; he was merely curious, and it was his curiosity that had nearly killed him. Kajiro remembered the words of his late opponent, something about the confounded animal and drowning him.

Then he understood it. The purpose of descending was not necessarily to reach the sea, but to reach something at the base of the cliffs.

He rushed over to the edge and looked down. But he could see little beyond Raiko's ledge, for this part of the cliff bulged slightly in the middle. If he wanted to see what was hidden at the base, he would have to make the descent himself. It was not a pleasant thought. What if another stranger, an ally of the dead man, were to arrive on the scene? His rope could be easily cut at any time during his descent or return.

Still undecided, he peered down once more. He heard a thin, wailing sound. He had heard this sound several times earlier, and he had thought it was the cry of sea gulls, because he was expecting to hear sea gulls. But now he strained his ears to listen for something different. And he heard a difference. Several varieties of sea gulls were to be found on this coast, and they had very different cries. But now he couldn't get the idea out of his head that the sound might be human, might be made by a girl weeping. Yuri! Could it be Yuri?

Chapter 9

By afternoon, neither Yuri nor the ronin had returned. Despite herself, Sada kept thinking of the words of the old lord. The ogres wanted red meat, he had said. They enjoyed cat meat, but they preferred tender human flesh. Of course he was a madman babbling nonsense. But Sada could not control a growing sense of dread. She had to do something.

Her husband would not permit her to send a large search party. "It would seriously weaken the garrison and the guards around the exile," he said firmly. "Besides, Yuri often goes out searching for her cat. They'll return when the cat grows tired of the game."

Sada was surprised by her husband's unprecedented firmness. She was on the point of issuing orders in defiance of his stand, but drew back on the brink of an open break with him. This was no time to make her husband lose face in public. Besides, what he had said about weakening the garrison was reasonable.

"Very well, then, I'll go myself," she announced. "Gorobei can lead a troop of men to accompany me."

Her guest made a suggestion. "I can go with you. Gorobei is needed more back here."

Sada was doubtful. "Are you sure you're

well enough? I wouldn't want you to have a relapse."

"I'm quite well enough to stay on a horse," declared the guest. "Mild exercise is good for me. I'll get stiff if I don't move a little."

They set out with a dozen men, all that the commander would allow them to take. It was a small escort, and not strong enough to defend Sada against a real enemy attack. But of course on this compact little island, no enemy force of any size could have arrived undetected.

Riding at the head of the procession with her guest, Sada found that she could actually be enjoying the outing, if it hadn't been for her anxiety over Yuri. Perhaps her husband was right. Yuri and Raiko would return when they became hungry enough. Meanwhile, this was her opportunity to have the fresh air and exercise that she had been too busy to get in recent weeks. She was also cheered by the obvious improvement in her guest, who was taking an active hand again. Perhaps her invitation to him had not been such a disastrous mistake after all.

"Where do you think we should search first?" he asked.

She knew the answer. Yuri had been reported going to the fishing village, and that would be the first place the ronin would search. The farm village would be another place he would naturally want to check. He had been attacked there, and he had heard strange sounds, sounds of someone eating noisily. For an instant, the image conjured by this thought was so horrible that Sada swallowed convulsively. But she controlled her panic. The ronin had not returned to report. The likelihood was that he had found no traces of Yuri at either the harbor or the farm village.

That left only one other obvious choice. "The convent," she said.

"Yes, the convent," agreed the guest. "Other than your mansion, it's the only place on the island large enough to hide . . . people."

The slight hesitation did not escape her. "Do you think the missing animals might be hidden there? But we've searched the place twice already, and pretty thoroughly, too. A watchdog is hard to keep out of sight!"

"I think I know what has happened to the missing animals," said the guest slowly. "I want to test my theory."

It was midafternoon when they arrived at the gate of the convent. When no one answered their call, Sada nearly lost her patience. She was tempted to have some of her men break down the gate, and was only restrained by fear of offending the abbess, her great-aunt.

The gate finally opened, and a black-robed young nun shuffled into view. She stood in the opening, making no move to invite them in.

Sada and her guest dismounted. "My sister cannot be found, and we should like to know if she is here," she said.

The nun's face was lowered, and it was

134

shadowed by the branches of a nearby pine tree. A light breeze moved the branches, causing the shadows to shift over her face. Her lips and jaw gave the impression of constantly changing shape. "I'm sorry, but Lady Yuri is no longer here," she said. "She came earlier this morning, and left when she didn't find her cat here."

Sada knew that in the face of the denial, pushing their way in would be insulting to the convent—and to her great-aunt. "Let me speak to the abbess, then," she said.

"The abbess has already retired, I'm afraid," said the nun, continuing to bar the way. "She is sleeping deeply, and would not be happy at being disturbed."

The guest moved up to the gate. "Perhaps you will allow us at least to look for Lady Yuri's cat. It may be hiding in some dark corner of the kitchen."

"I'm sorry," said the nun. "Such a search would be disturbing to her ladyship, the abbess."

"How can it, if she is sleeping as deeply as you said?" the guest said quickly. "We'll make very little noise, I assure you."

Sada caught his eye and gave a signal to her men. Without quite resorting to force, they pushed past the nun and through the gate. "Which is the way to the kitchen?" demanded Sada.

The nun recovered herself and bowed. "I will have someone conduct you." Before Sada could stop her, she turned and rushed off. There was something ridiculous in the way she hurried, taking tiny little steps.

The guest looked thoughtfully at the running nun.

"Silly woman!" muttered Sada. She had a suspicion that the nun had hurried off to warn someone, or was simply being obstructive. Impatient to begin her search, Sada looked around the courtyard, feeling the oppressiveness of the place. Now she could understand Yuri's reluctance to be sent here.

As her small party stood exposed in the middle of the courtyard, Sada sensed that many eyes were studying her, her guest, and her men. She could see a few dark, indistinct shapes on the covered walks along the sides of the courtyard. Most of the nuns lurked in the shadows, barely visible. Only two of them were in full sight, and like the young nun at the gate, they had heavy, coarse features. Sada could not imagine her fastidious sister joining a community of women such as these.

Even her soldiers were beginning to look uneasy. One of them spoke up. "My lady, we don't have to wait for someone to conduct us. I know the way to the kitchen."

Sada turned to him eagerly. "That's right! You were on the last search here."

As they followed the soldier, Sada asked him whether anything looked different this time. The man hesitated. "Well, almost all the nuns stayed out of sight last time. This afternoon, some of them seemed to have got over their shyness."

On entering the kitchen, the first thing that struck them was the smell. This was explained by a brown, viscous mass of fermented soy beans spilled on a counter. One of the nuns was trying to scoop it up again into a bowl. The fermented beans were used as a rice chaser and a valuable source of protein for the vegetarian nuns, but they had a pungent smell that lingered in the kitchen, in the dining hall, and even on the chopsticks long after the meal was finished.

Sada's guest did not join the search. As the soldiers looked into cupboards, behind the stove, and into food bins, he stood gazing at the nun who was cleaning up the spill. "Strange," he murmured softly, and only Sada was close enough to hear him. "According to our friend, the ronin, some pickled radishes were spilled while he was searching. They are unusually clumsy and careless with food here, although religious houses generally have to live frugally."

"Is that why you wanted Yuri's cat along on the search?" Sada whispered. "Raiko's nose would detect something underneath the smell of the fermented beans?"

The guest nodded. "It's a pity he isn't along."

After the soldiers reported on the failure of their search, the guest asked to see the kitchen knives and cleavers.

"They're dirty, and they have to be washed," muttered one of the nuns.

"I don't mind soiling my hands," replied the guest amiably.

The nun hesitated for a moment, and then went to fetch the knives. She held out three of them, a thick cleaver and two slicing knives.

The guest ran his finger along the blade of the cleaver and closely scrutinized the edge. A samurai, who understands sword blades, can also read the most minute scratch and nick on a kitchen knife. Sada, following the guest's moving finger, saw what he had been looking at: several tiny notches in the edge. Finally the guest put down the knife, took out a piece of rice paper tissue, and wiped his finger. "Yes, you're right. The knives are dirty."

No trace of the cat was found in the kitchen, and the search party started to leave. In the courtyard, the guest turned suddenly to Sada. "Ask one of your men to run quickly to the gate."

"You want him to hurry back to the mansion?" asked Sada.

"No, just have him run to the gate and wait," said the guest. "Some of the nuns will probably try to run after him. If they do, watch their feet!"

Mystified, Sada summoned one of her soldiers and briskly gave her orders. If the man was as mystified as his mistress, he gave no sign. Nodding, he turned and began running. For a couple of seconds, there was no sound in the courtyard except the crunching of his feet pounding on the fine gravel.

Then Sada heard a low murmur around her, and the courtyard exploded into activity. Several black-robed figures went flying after the soldier. They caught up with him before he reached the gate. They made no attempt to lay hands on him, but stood solidly blocking his way. Obeying Sada's orders, the soldier did not try to break out, and merely waited.

Sada had been watching the feet of the pursuing nuns. They had not run like the nun at the gate earlier, who had moved in tiny, mincing steps. These nuns took large strides, and in their hurry, forgot to turn their toes inward, as women do.

Shaken, Sada turned to her guest. "Yes, I see what you mean. These are not real nuns."

The guest was looking around at the black-robed nuns, gathering in throngs under the covered walkways surrounding the courtyard. He was very pale, and the dismay on his face was plain to see. "I'm afraid I've made a serious miscalculation about their numbers," he said bitterly. "We're in great danger here."

Before Sada could reply, a nun approached and bowed. "Please accept some tea in the study of the scriptures reading hall."

Sada opened her mouth to refuse, but the guest forestalled her. "Thank you. Lady Sada appreciates your hospitality."

"We're badly outnumbered," whispered the

guest to Sada, as they followed their guide across the courtyard. "We have to bluff our way out."

At the hall, Sada's soldiers stood in a file outside while she and the guest were invited to seat themselves on the straw cushions in the room. Thanking her guide, Sada managed to preserve a calm and gracious exterior, but her heart was beating fast. The cavernous room, with its polished floor of dark wood and its two rows of thick pillars, did not add to her comfort.

At first Sada thought they were alone in the room, but a rustle from a corner of the dark room drew her eyes. A hooded nun was seated with her back to them. Slowly, she turned around, and on her coarse-featured face was a broad smile.

"I had the pleasure of entertaining your sister earlier, Lady Sada," said the nun. "Imagine my delight at having you here as well—and you've even brought a guest!"

"I'm afraid we can't stay," the guest said quietly. "It's late, and Lady Sada's husband will be worried about her safety. In fact he may even come with his men to investigate."

The nun continued to smile. "Oh, but I'm sure we can send a message to calm his fears. I shall attend to that right away."

Sada took a deep breath. "It's more complicated than that. You see, because of some instructions I left behind, the health of an important personage staying with us will be seriously affected if I don't return by a certain time."

For what seemed like an eternity, the nun stared blankly at her. Sada wondered if she had made a mistake. Even if she hadn't made a mistake, would her bluff work? She glanced at her guest, and was glad to read vigorous approval in his eyes.

Suddenly the nun began to chuckle. "Oh my, you're right! It is complicated, isn't it? I'm too stupid to understand what you are saying about the health of your important personage. But at least I can see that you are anxious to be gone. Therefore I will not press my invitation on you."

Neither Sada nor her guest spent time on more than a minimum of polite regrets as they took their leave. Outside, her men were standing at attention, and she could see relief even in the set of their shoulders when she gave orders to leave.

By the time they crossed the front courtyard again, it was late afternoon, and the sun cast long shadows across the stone-paved path. Sada had the eerie sensation that a great many more of the nuns were now hovering in the walkways and lurking behind the pillars around them. Her guest was right: They were badly outnumbered.

Her men also seemed to sense a vague threat in the motionless black shapes surrounding them. "Look!" said one of the soldiers. "There are a lot more of these nuns than before! You'd think they had the magical power to multiply themselves!"

As Sada and her men made haste to reach the gate of the convent, she half expected a forward surge from the "nuns." But they were allowed to proceed without interference. Once outside the gate, they set out for home at full speed.

Sada knew that she had to inform her husband instantly about her discovery. It was vitally important for the commander to know that the convent was occupied by strangers, by men who had somehow arrived undetected on the island. She could not resist looking back half a dozen times to see if any of the strangers came after them. There was no pursuit, however.

Although relieved at leaving, Sada was not entirely at ease. True, the "nuns" had been reluctant to let them go, but neither did they seem unduly disturbed at having to release Sada and her party. Weren't they worried that she might carry back the news of her discovery to the commander? It was as if Sada's movements were no longer of great consequence. She hated the idea.

Chapter 10

Kajiro knew what he had to do. There was no avoiding it. He had to lower himself down to the base of the cliff. "Raiko," he said to the cat, quite seriously, "I'm leaving you to stand guard here."

Again he tied the loose end of the rope around his waist, and made sure that his sword was in a position for an easy draw. Then he began to lower himself down the cliff once more. This time he descended faster than before, and he could feel the cloth of his mittens wearing out. I hope I won't have to make many more of these descents, he thought.

After he passed Raiko's old ledge, his arms began to ache, another sign that he was still out of condition. Although, everything considered, he was doing better than he had hoped.

The noise of the pounding waves grew louder, but so did the wailing sound. He became more and more certain that the voice was human. After a while the wailing stopped, and he was soon able to distinguish something like speaking voices. They were definitely feminine. His hopes rose, and he forgot the ache in his arms. Toward the end he was almost sliding, and his palms burned as the mittens gave way entirely.

His feet hit the rocks with a bump. Recovering from his jarring, he realized that the voices had stopped. All he could hear now was the sound of the sea. Had he imagined the voices?

He looked around, searching the narrow, rocky shore. Already he was drenched from the waves dashing against the base of the cliff. There was hardly enough room to stand on the slippery rocks. The sunlight, scattered by the droplets of water, bounced against the rocks in thousands of colorful gems.

Then his startled eyes caught sight of a strange vision: several slender figures slowly rose from behind the rocks. Partly obscured by the spray, they seemed to float, like the legless ghosts of the drowned.

One of the figures rushed forward, and the voice of Yuri said, "What kept you?"

Wet and shivering, she wore the same expression as Raiko when he found the cat on the ledge. Kajiro could only grin foolishly at her.

"You can laugh," Yuri cried, "but I've been here for hours!" She burst into tears.

Kajiro stepped forward, wanting to take her into his arms and comfort her. But he stopped. She might find him presumptuous. One of the other figures moved forward and put an arm around the sobbing girl. Kajiro saw that it was a slender woman with a shaven head.

His amazement grew as he looked at the other figures around him. Except for Yuri, they all had shaven heads, slightly darkened by a short, black fuzz. He was surrounded by nuns.

"Who . . . who were the people in the convent, then?" he asked.

Yuri had recovered herself. "They were men! They disguised themselves as nuns! I don't know why we didn't notice!"

Once he got over the surprise, Kajiro realized that all along there had been clues to the true nature of the "nuns," if only he had been alert enough to see them. The untidy heaps of bedding in the cupboards, for instance. Men would have considered it beneath their dignity to air quilts and fold mattresses neatly.

One of the nuns suggested that they get out of the spray first before continuing the discussion. The nuns all had ageless, unlined faces, but this one had an authoritative air indicating seniority. She led the way, stepping carefully among the rocks.

The day had held so many unexpected developments that Kajiro thought nothing more could surprise him. He was wrong. The nuns stopped in front of a huge black hole in the base of the cliff, and to his amazement Kajiro saw a grotto, a natural cave.

The mouth of the grotto was invisible from the sea because of tall rocks in front of it. From above, it was screened by the overhanging cliff. It was an ideal hiding place.

But as a residence, the grotto lacked comfort. Looking around the cheerless chamber, now getting dark, Kajiro could see only a few reed mats to protect the inhabitants from the damp.

Yuri saw his glance. "As you can gather, we didn't exactly choose to stay here," she said. "I've been here for only a couple of hours, and I'm cold through and through. These poor nuns have been here for more than a week!"

Although the nuns wore the same dark robes as the false nuns in the convent, their slight build made them look more than ever like wraiths in the dim light of the cave. Their faces were wan and pale, almost ethereal. What their suffering was, Kajiro could only guess. "Don't they give you enough to eat?" he asked.

The oldest of the nuns smiled gently—the smile was a world apart from the toothy, almost feral smiles of the "nuns" up in the convent. "We get a daily ration of food, just barely enough to keep us from starvation."

One of the other nuns, a young one who looked no older than Yuri, was sniffling. "And if any of us tried to shout or cried too loudly, they would cut our rations in half."

"They must be barbarians!" said Kajiro. Nevertheless, he thought, the men who had taken over the convent could have simply slaughtered the inhabitants. It was much more troublesome and risky to lower the nuns, one by one into the cave, and supply them daily with food.

The older nuns must have read his thoughts. "No, these men are not barbarians. They are conspirators, and they have their orders to carry out. But murdering innocent nuns is against their principles—for I believe that they do have principles."

Kajiro had to agree. The false nuns had not killed Yuri when they had had her in their power. They might attack him, an armed man—they even tried to drown Raiko—but they did not murder defenseless women.

"All right," he said, "what are these men planning to do? What are their orders?"

"I have a pretty good idea," said Yuri.

On reflection, so did Kajiro. The exile—these men must have come to rescue the old, exiled daimyo right from under the noses of the garrison. He had to admire the audacity of the plan.

"But how did all these men get here?" he asked. "The island has only the one harbor at the fishing village, and it's watched day and night."

Then he saw it. The stout rope tied to a pine tree could be used not only for climbing down the cliff, it could also be used for climbing up. "So," he mused, "the men must have arrived by ones and twos, and at night, when they could not be seen as they rowed around the island. They landed on the far side, where no one would think of looking."

"They must have hidden themselves in the grotto at first," said Yuri. "When enough of them got here, they broke into the convent and occupied it."

"Is the abbess part of the plot?" asked Kajiro.

"Of course not!" said Yuri, affronted. Her great-aunt might not inspire love, but she was a relative, after all.

"The abbess dared not speak out to the commander's searchers," explained the nun. "She was afraid of endangering our safety."

"How did you find us?" Yuri asked Kajiro. "My sister's men missed this place completely."

Her voice was warm with admiration, and for a moment Kajiro was overcome with shyness. "It was Raiko," he said. "He led me to the pine tree, and I saw the rope coiled there."

"Raiko!" cried Yuri. "He's safe? When those horrible men were lowering me down the cliff, I heard some yowling and some curses. I thought they killed him!"

"He's too tough for them," Kajiro said quickly. The girl was close to tears again. "I left him on guard at the top of the cliff. If we don't go up soon, he'll be hungry again."

He looked around the cave. There were some fifteen nuns altogether. Some were sitting, listless from hunger and despair, but most had got up and were listening eagerly, hopefully. How could he possibly pull them up the cliff one by one? Moreover, he might be attacked by men from the convent during the rescue.

Again the older nun was able to read his thoughts. "You must go immediately and warn the garrison." She managed a smile. "We can wait. Perhaps you can send boats for us later. Being lowered down that sheer cliff was a terrifying experience. Going up the cliff is more than we are able to do in our weakened condition."

"I'm climbing up the cliff with you," declared Yuri.

Kajiro looked at her slender, delicate hands. "I'm afraid not, Lady Yuri. It's a long, hard climb."

"I can climb part of the way, and you can pull me the rest of the way," said Yuri. Before Kajiro could object again, she added, "I can warn the men at the garrison, while you go to the harbor for boats to rescue these nuns. Besides, Raiko needs me."

Matsuzo was seasick. It was humiliating but true. He had a tendency toward seasickness, and it was always worse when his stomach was empty. If he had asked the boatman for something to eat before setting out, he wouldn't have been brought so low. Now it was too late.

"How much farther do we have to go?" he asked.

"Only a little bit more," said the boatman. "Look, you can make out the houses of the fishermen now."

Matsuzo sat up and looked toward the island, but quickly closed his eyes when the boat gave a sudden lurch. "How was my friend when you left him?" He asked after a while, trying to distract his mind from his misery.

"He was in better shape than you," said the boatman, grinning. With his head bent to one

149

side, he looked sardonic. "When I saw him last, he was walking steadily enough."

Cheered by the news, Matsuzo risked another look at the island. They were much closer now, and he could clearly see the houses grouped around the harbor, the curved beach, and some half a dozen boats resting on the sand. Behind the boats were some human figures in motion—in very violent motion. Matsuzo realized that he was witnessing a fight.

The boatman had seen the fighting as well, and he stopped rowing. "Do you want me to go on?" he asked.

Matsuzo considered. If they returned to the mainland, they might also encounter violence, and in conditions less favorable to them. Here at least they could join the fight and help the right side—if only they knew which was the right side. "Let's land," he said. At the prospect of a good fight, his seasickness disappeared.

The boatman began to row hard. Soon they were close enough to shore for Matsuzo to see that the fight was uneven, and one side was getting much the worse of it. Who was winning, friend or foe?

The boatman gave him the answer. "I'm afraid the men getting the upper hand are the conspirators. I recognize that man over there."

They had been sighted from the beach. Now that the uneven fight was nearly over, some of the victors were wading toward the boat.

Matsuzo had to decide quickly. Should he

pretend to be one of the conspirators, and then make his escape afterward? Would he sound plausible enough?

But the decision was not his to make. "I'm afraid they remember me," said the boatman. With his crooked neck, he was hard to forget. "That man saw me on the mainland when I was helping your friend into the boat."

Even if they had wanted to turn the boat around, it was too late. A surge carried their boat straight toward two men waiting for them on the shore.

"I wish I had my sword," muttered Matsuzo.

"There's a spare oar behind you," said the boatman "It's the best I can do, I'm afraid."

Matsuzo barely had time to raise the oar before the men were on them. One man slashed out with his sword. Matsuzo swerved, swung his oar like a wooden practice sword, finding its extra length an unexpected asset. But its heavier weight caused the swing to fall lower than he had intended. The oar took his attacker on the thigh instead of the torso. The man grunted and sank to knees in the water, just as the boatman swung the boat sharply. The keel struck the attacker in the head, and he went under.

Matsuzo was already out of the boat and engaged with the second attacker. This man was a better swordsman than the first one, but Matsuzo, fired with the desire to pay the conspirators back for the discomforts of the last few days, was too powerful for him. He had got the feel of the oar now, and brought it down with the full force of his anger and frustration behind it. His opponent's sword, coming up to parry, was knocked out his hand. Stunned and disarmed, the man didn't even see the boatman swing his anchor at him. As the man fell, Matsuzo snatched quickly and retrieved his sword from the water. Armed at last, Matsuzo and boatman now had time to assess the situation on the beach.

One faction, the losing side in the fight, consisted of men wearing more or less identical clothes. They were almost certainly soldiers of the garrison. Only three of them were still on their feet, while some five or six had been struck down.

The attackers were less uniformly clothed, and it seemed that there had been more of them from the very beginning. Matsuzo estimated them to be nearly twenty in number, counting their fallen. They must have overwhelmed the soldiers on guard duty at the harbor. It was a mystery how the conspirators had succeeded in landing such a force on the island unobserved.

Matsuzo had no time to puzzle over the mystery, for several of the conspirators were now rushing at him. He ran quickly up the beach to one of the cottages and turned to face his attackers. At least he now had the wall of the house protecting his back.

One of the attackers lunged. Matsuzo took advantage of the man's clumsy footwork to block his attack before the lunge could attain its full momentum. His parry sent the attacker reeling back, and Matsuzo was already swinging at a second man who was just beginning to raise his sword.

His intensive apprenticeship under Zenta had transformed him from an ardent beginner to a formidable swordsman. In time he might even become an outstanding one—if he survived long enough.

Now that Matsuzo's attackers had a measure of his caliber, they became more cautious. Their numbers increased as more and more of the conspirators realized that the newcomer was a greater threat than the exhausted soldiers.

Kimi's brother, where was he? He was no longer in sight. Had he run away, or had he been struck down? Matsuzo hoped that the boatman had the sense to run for help. Surely one of the soldiers or fishermen had already gone to alert the garrison? But he was afraid that even if more soldiers arrived, it would be too late for himself and the remaining soldiers on the beach.

Help came in a startling form. Out of the sky, a dark cloud dropped on his attackers and threw them to the ground.

Panting, Matsuzo stood amazed and stared at the huge, heaving mass at his feet. Occasionally an arm or a leg poked out and waved in the air. Grunts and curses issued from the thrashing bundle. Matsuzo realized that the dark cloud was a thick stack of fishnets.

Warily, a number of fishermen emerged from behind their cottages. Armed with sticks and oars, they rained practiced blows on the men trapped under the nets. For practiced they were, in clubbing tuna, bonito, and the occasional baby shark they caught in their nets.

"We have to hurry, before they tear our nets to pieces," said one of the fishermen to Matsuzo.

Since the fishermen had the situation well in hand, Matsuzo turned his eyes to the struggle farther up the beach. Things were not going well for the soldiers. Only two remained standing, and they both looked nearly spent. Already most of the attackers were looking around to make sure that there were no other survivors. On catching sight of Matsuzo, they shouted, pointing.

Matsuzo braced himself. He was one man against a dozen, and he knew that the trick with the fishnets could not be repeated.

But the rush against him had barely begun before he heard more shouting, and some of his attackers drew back to look at a figure that had appeared on the path leading out of the village.

Matsuzo's heart leaped, but his hopes were dashed when he saw that the man was not dressed in the dark uniform of the soldiers. He was another conspirator.

But no, he wasn't! Some of the conspirators were running at him with raised swords. Who could it be? Did he represent some third party on this baffling island?

**

Kajiro was still worried about Yuri. He felt guilty about letting her return alone to the mansion—alone except for Raiko. The cat had proved himself to be a stalwart fighter once already, but even he was no match for an armed ambush.

Yuri had insisted that an ambush was very unlikely. She was the one who had to go to the mansion, because her words would carry more weight with the garrison than his. He was a stranger, after all, and he would have a hard time convincing the commander to take the drastic step of ordering an all-out attack on the convent.

There was no help for it. Yuri had to be the one to warn the men at the garrison. She had also insisted that he should go straight to the harbor and secure boats for the nuns. Remembering the pitiful faces of the nuns, who were trying to smile bravely, Kajiro knew that he had to rescue them from their wretched prison as soon as possible.

At least the fishermen would be eager to help. They were friendly, unlike the farmers, and they seemed unshakably loyal to Yuri's family. If he asked for boats, all the available ones would be at his service.

A short distance front the harbor, he saw a man running toward him. As the runner came closer, he noticed that the man had a crooked neck. He was dressed as a boatman, Kajiro was glad to see. Perhaps the man could arrange for some boats.

Before Kajiro could say a word, the boatman yelped with fright on seeing him, and ran off the path into some tall reeds. Bewildered, Kajiro watched the man with the crooked neck scramble frantically through the reeds. Why was he so frightened?

Continuing on his way, Kajiro was able to go faster, for the path now descended steeply to the shore. The harbor soon came into view, and before he had gone another dozen steps, he heard shouts. Coming to a stop at the edge of the village, he stared at the fighting on the beach below him. One man was fighting a dozen attackers. Although surrounded, he seemed to be holding his own.

One of the attackers saw Kajiro and pointed excitedly at him. There were some shouts, and suddenly two of the men rushed at him with their swords raised. Kajiro had no time to call out, to explain. His reflexes took over, and his sword was out in a flash. At least his reflexes were regaining their former speed. With the advantage of rushing downhill, he took the first attacker in the throat before the man's sword could even descend. The second attacker was shaken, and his hesitated too long. Kajiro's sword cut him down before he could recover himself.

The fighting on the beach froze. Clearly Kajiro's arrival had taken everyone by surprise.

What he had to do now was join forces with the lone fighter, whoever he was. One's enemy's enemy had to be an ally. He liked the looks of this ally, a young samurai who fought with a coolness that made light of the odds against him.

Kajiro's aim was to get himself closer to this young fighter, so that they could protect each other's back. The other man evidently had the same idea. Before the men surrounding him had recovered from the surprise of the newcomer's arrival, the young samurai made a slashing attack, and in the next instant he had broken out of the encirclement. In half a dozen rapid strides he was at Kajiro's side. The two men exchanged a quick nod of acknowledgment, and turned to face their attackers.

Their situation was now less desperate, but they were still badly outnumbered. The two of them were surrounded by eleven men, eleven good swordsmen, for the weaker fighters had already fallen.

Kajiro was tiring fast. His day had been strenuous, and his arms were still aching from climbing up and down and up and down cliffs. He even had to pull Yuri during his last climb. His ally's last parry was just a bit slow, and he narrowly escaped a vicious slash. After all, the younger man had been fighting much longer.

Their attackers must have sensed that the two men were beginning to flag, for the attacks now stepped up in tempo. Kajiro was afraid that he would not last much longer.

A hideous yowl cut through the air. Several of the attackers jumped back. Kajiro himself nearly dropped his sword in surprise, and he at least knew what had made the noise. Raiko! How had he gotten here?

Before anyone could recover from the unearthly yell, a door behind Kajiro opened and a voice hissed, "Inside! Quickly!"

His new ally could certainly move fast. The young samurai hurtled through the door, pulling Kajiro after him. The door crashed shut, nearly catching one of their attackers' swords. The fisherman, who had opened the door for them, quickly slammed the stout wooden crossbar into place.

When Kajiro recovered from the surprise, he began to laugh. "This was the second time today I was rescued by a cat! I hope Raiko hasn't come to any harm."

"That was not a cat," said the fisherman, grinning, "That was my son."

From behind a folding screen, a small head with a huge smile showed for an instant. Some convincing mews and some less convincing purrs sounded, showing that the boy's imitation of Raiko was not limited to angry yowls.

Meanwhile, the young samurai had sheathed his sword and was straightening his clothes. "Please forgive my lack of manners and allow me to introduce myself," he said, bowing formally. "My name is Ishihara Matsuzo. May I know whom I have the honor of addressing?"

Before Kajiro could speak, the fisherman said, "This gentleman is the famous warrior Konishi Zenta!"

Matsuzo stared. "But Zenta is a good friend of mine, and I have never seen this man before in my life!"

Chapter 11

Sada knew that something was wrong even before she was inside the gate of the mansion. She found the men of the garrison milling confusedly in the front courtyard, and it was some time before they even noticed her return.

"Where is Gorobei?" she asked a soldier who stood wringing his hands.

"It's a disaster, my lady!" he moaned. "A total disaster!"

"Where—is—Gorobei?" she repeated, enunciating her words slowly and clearly, as if talking to a deaf man.

"H-he h-has gone to look for Lady Yuri," stammered the man. "When she didn't come back, he became worried."

Sada's hands clenched. She knew of Gorobei's interest in Yuri, but to rush off to search for her was an act of irresponsibility. He would have to be demoted. The trouble was, he was by far the most able man in the garrison.

She turned to her guest, and found that he was already moving off toward the inner apartments. Sobs and agitated voices could be heard from that direction. Then she knew. She hurried after her guest. "It's the exile isn't it? Something has happened to him!"

The scene in the exile's suite confirmed her

fears. By the door lay the four guards, all slain, while inside were the two maids who served as attendants to the old man. Both girls were weeping hysterically. The exile's bed was empty. There was no sign of him.

Sada seized one of the girls and slapped her hard. "What happened?" she demanded.

The girl's sobs hiccupped to a stop. "He said . . . he . . . he could summon the ogres! And they came! They k-killed the guards and to-took him away!"

The guest turned to the other girl. "Is this true?"

His quiet, level voice had a calming effect on her. "Y-Yes, it's true," she said.

"We were preparing the old lord for bed," said the first girl, the talkative one, "when we heard one of the guards cry out. Then the door opened, and four monstrous ogres came in."

"What did they look like?" demanded Sada sharply. "How did you know they were ogres?" The peasants on the island might believe in ogres, but her maids should have known better.

"Oh, my lady," moaned the talkative girl, "they had fangs and huge, round eyes!"

"Did you see them too?" Sada asked the other girl. The girl nodded.

"And I saw horns!" cried the talkative girl. "They had horns sticking out on top of their heads!"

Sada frowned as she studied the girl. Surely she was making up the part about the horns?

But the girl seemed to believe what she was saying. Then Sada remembered something: The ronin had claimed that his attacker in the farm village had horns.

"Did the ogres speak at all?" asked the guest.

"No," said the girl. "They just bowed to the old lord. He laughed and went away with them!"

Further questioning could not shake the girl's story. The other girl, the silent one, nodded corroboration.

"I'd better see what my fine husband was doing while all this was going on," Sada said between her teeth. The commander had the ultimate responsibility here at the garrison for anything that went wrong.

Sada and her guest found the commander at his desk, writing a poem. This was too much for Sada. She wanted to throw the ink slab at him. "Don't you know what's happened?" she hissed. "Don't you even care?"

The commander put down his brush and looked up calmly at her. "Yes, I know that the exile is gone. And since the responsibility is mine, I'm ready to commit hara-kiri. I've just been writing my death poem."

Exasperation rose in Sada like molten lava. "Don't be ridiculous! This is no time for joking!"

"I'm not joking," protested her husband. "When I make a joke, it's funnier than this."

The guest cleared his throat. "Sir, it may not be necessary for you to commit hara-kiri. If we move quickly enough, we may be able to recapture the exile before he leaves the island."

"The convent!" exclaimed Sada. "Those nuns must be hiding him!"

For once the commander was shaken out of his calm. "Surely not? Those pious nuns wouldn't do anything like that!"

"If they are nuns, then I'm the shogun's wet-nurse," said the guest. "Yes, those so-called nuns are behind this."

"We must order an all-out attack on the convent," declared Sada.

A faint perturbation rippled across the commander's smooth brow. "Are you sure that's wise? What would the abbess say?"

Before Sada could answer, the door opened abruptly and a maid thrust her head in. "Lady Yuri is back, and she says she has some important news!"

The barely suppressed excitement in the maid's voice should have prepared Sada, but she was still stunned at the sight of her younger sister.

Since early childhood, Yuri had always had a troublesome tendency to run as freely as a boy. All too often had Sada's patience been sorely tried by her sister's disheveled appearance after a day's carefree romping. Things would have been different if their mother hadn't died when Yuri was a child. Their late father, instead of being firm with the younger girl, had encouraged her boyish behavior.

Even after her sister's worst escapades, however, Sada had never seen her look quite so bedraggled. Yuri's long hair was tumbling loose over her shoulders—that, at least, was a familiar sight. What shocked Sada was the dirt. Yuri's fingers were so begrimed that they looked like claws. A wide streak of dirt covered most of her left cheek, and her clothes were filthy rags, literally rags. Sada found herself beyond anger. She wanted to laugh, hysterically.

But she sobered when she saw the expression on Yuri's face. "What happened?" she asked sharply. "Has someone molested you?"

Yuri shook her head impatiently. "Not in the way you mean. I was captured by those so-called nuns. Did you know that they are really men in disguise?"

"We know that now," said Sada. "But where did they hide you? We were just searching the convent ourselves!"

Yuri began to describe her adventures from the beginning. Sada's amazement mounted as she heard about the grotto under the cliffs. Even the guest, who normally had such control over his emotions, started at the mention of the hidden cave. "So that was it! That was why I underestimated the number of invaders in the convent! I thought most of the figures I saw there were the real nuns, terrorized into keeping silent. After all, where on the island can you hide fifteen grown women? That's why I got such an appalling shock in the courtyard when I saw that *all* the figures in black were men! I didn't realize that they had hidden away the real nuns in the grotto!"

Sada felt a sinking sensation in her chest. "So we don't know how many of the conspirators have arrived. We may already have a full-scale invasion on our hands!"

"Where is the ronin who rescued you?" the guest asked Yuri.

"He's gone to the harbor to see about some boats" replied Yuri.

"What!" cried the guest, jumping to his feet. He turned to Sada. "The boats! Of course! That's how the exile can escape from the island!"

"But . . ." Sada thought back to the ronin's face. "Do you think he could be one of the plotters?"

"After all, what do we know about him?" asked the guest. "We don't even know his real name."

"I thought you agreed that he was harmless," Sada reminded him.

Her guest grimaced. "I'm not infallible! I made disastrous mistake in underestimating the number of the invaders, and it was only by your quick thinking that we got away from the convent. I could be wrong about this ronin too."

"But he rescued me!" protested Yuri. "Raiko likes him!"

Sada looked closely at her sister. "I suppose this means *you* like him. What about Gorobei?"

Yuri turned red at the mention of Gorobei,

although the color was not easily seen under all the dirt. Her chin went up. "Gorobei doesn't really care for me."

"I agree with Yuri about Gorobei," the commander said mildly. He was the only person who looked completely undisturbed. "Gorobei is not interested in Yuri, only in her position. This ronin, whoever he is, is more trustworthy."

Again Sada's fingers itched to throw the ink slab at her husband. "Let's postpone our discussion of Yuri's alleged suitors for the moment, shall we?" she snarled. "We have to decide where to send our main force. To the convent, or to the harbor?"

"To the convent, of course," said Yuri. "We *know* that the plotters are making it their headquarters, and we know they arrived by climbing the cliffs. We might even catch them trying to land more men."

"Yes," mused Sada, "they might smuggle the old lord off the island by lowering him down the cliff, the way they lowered you and the nuns. They'd have a boat waiting below for him."

"The boats are the key," said the guest. "Gaining control of all the boats on the island would prevent the garrison from setting out in pursuit. I think your men must go to make sure of the harbor first."

"To the harbor, then," said Sada, convinced. "Let's order the men to start immediately."

Her husband coughed. "Someone should stay behind at the mansion. We have strong defenses here, and we must not leave the place to the invaders."

Sada slowly turned and stared at him. Was he suggesting that he should remain behind, and stay out of the fighting at the harbor? An absentminded dreamer he might be, but she never expected him to be a coward.

To her surprise, the guest agreed with her husband. "The commander is right. If the invaders occupy the mansion, they can hold out against us for a long time. Your father built this place for its strong position."

"But we can't split our forces!" protested Sada. "We don't know how many men they have, and we have to be strong enough to secure the harbor at least." She looked at her husband. "If you want to stay here with the maids, you can. The rest of us will go to the harbor."

She did not even try to hide her contempt. But her husband looked unruffled. "What I suggest is that you and Yuri stay behind to organize the defense here, in the unlikely event that this should be necessary."

Sada's lower lip jutted out. "I'm going to the harbor with the fighting men. That's more important."

For the second time that day—for the second time since her marriage—her husband became unexpectedly stubborn. He insisted that as commander of the garrison, it was his duty to lead his men to the beach. Sada finally gave way when he pointed out that they were wasting valuable time by arguing. She was almost as surprised at herself for giving in as at her husband for being so insistent.

Yuri opened her mouth to protest on being told that she was to stay behind with her sister. Sada lost her patience. "Oh, do be quiet! Anyway, you need a bath!"

The sun was a low orange ball in the sky when Sada saw her husband setting off toward the harbor. In a remarkably short time, he had given the necessary orders, and now he was briskly leading the twenty-five armed men down the hill. Sada looked at the departing men, who represented the whole of the garrison, aside from the patrol already at the fishing village. She had not completely recovered from her astonishment at seeing her husband as a man of action. He seemed almost like a stranger. She was not altogether sure she didn't prefer the old poetic dreamer, who was at least easier to control. She glanced at her guest, standing next to her. He seemed equally bemused.

"Your husband can be quite decisive when he wants to be," murmured the guest.

Sada agreed. She had the feeling that events were moving too fast for her. Even more disturbing was the suspicion that she had overlooked something. She sighed and reentered the gate, for she had to make sure of the security of the mansion. It was now solely in the hands of herself and her women—and one convalescent guest.

But even the convalescent guest meant to desert her. "What Yuri said about the cliffs is sensible," said the guest, frowning. "I think I'd better go and have a look."

"You're leaving us too?" cried Sada.

"I'm sorry to abandon you like this," said the guest. "Anyway, in case of a fight here, I wouldn't do much good."

Sada did feel abandoned, and she couldn't suppress a spurt of resentment. But what he had said was reasonable. "Oh, very well," she muttered. "We can do without you."

Nevertheless, her eyes followed him as he walked in the direction of the convent. Soon he reached a turn in the path and disappeared from view.

At Matsuzo's words, Kajiro knew that his impersonation was over. He found it difficult to look at the fisherman and his son. But in a way, it was a relief to end the pretense, to be himself again. Having to live up to Zenta's reputation was a strain. Now he could relax, he could drink freely. Only the need to drink was no longer so strong—at least for now.

He stole a glance at the others. "My name is Itoh Kajiro," he said. "I didn't start out to impersonate your friend, but when my boatman and the local people mistook me for Zenta, I . . . well . . . I wanted to stay on the island, and I thought they would accept me more if they thought I was a famous swordsman."

The young samurai, Matsuzo, did not look particularly offended. In this age of turmoil, impersonating a famous warrior was not unknown, for it was a means of getting respect, hospitality, and the possibility of employment. After accepting Kajiro's confession in good part, he turned his attention back to the heavy thumps made by their attackers trying to break in.

It was the fisherman who looked most unhappy. "And I thought you were Zenta!" he said, bitterly disappointed. "I though that with you fighting for us, we'd be able to defeat them out there. Now what are we going to do?"

"Maybe my boatman has gone to the garrison for help," suggested Matsuzo hopefully. He looked at Kajiro. "Did you happen to meet a man with a crooked neck on your way here?"

Kajiro remembered the man who had scuttled off into the reeds at his approach. "Yes, come to think of it. I see now that he must have mistaken me for one of the invaders. He was probably on his way to the mansion for help, but now I'm afraid he'll be taking the long way around."

"That means we'll just have to hold them off a little longer," said Matsuzo. He winced as a loud boom was followed by a splintering noise. One section of the wall was beginning to weaken from the battering.

"Wait, this might hold them for a bit," said the fisherman, dragging up some ropes strung, with floats. They all helped him hang the tangle of ropes over the splintering wall. The ropes would not stop a rush completely, but the attackers would be momentarily entangled.

"I wonder what has happened to Zenta," said Matsuzo, frowning. "My boatman said he ferried him across four days ago. Where can he be?"

Kajiro had the glimmering of an idea. "Has your friend been sick?"

Matsuzo looked around. "He was wounded in a fight we had on the mainland—how badly, I don't know. But he was still determined to come to the island. The wife of the commander here sent him a message saying she needed his help. He used to be a friend of her family's."

"I see now," said Kajiro. He felt a tide of embarrassment wash over him. "No wonder Lady Sada laughed when I was presented to her as Zenta! The real Zenta was right here under her roof!"

"You've seen him?" Matsuzo asked quickly. "How is he?"

Before Kajiro could answer, the wall broke open with a crash. As the fisherman had hoped, the fishing tackle provided the all-important delay. The four attackers were entangled, and while they tried wildly to free themselves, the defenders made short work of them.

Expecting other attackers to follow, Kajiro peered out and was surprised to see that the rest of the invaders were all down near the beach. "Look!" he pointed. "They're taking the boats!"

***

Sada paced restlessly up and down the main room of the mansion. Like most women in samurai families, she was trained in arms, especially in the use of the long-handled halberd. She had one in her hand now, and her hair was tied back with a headband to hold it in place in case she had to fight.

The dividing panels of the room had been removed at her orders, so that she would have a clear view. Seated in the room were Yuri and four of the serving women who had been trained to fight. They were all armed with halberds.

"I feel like a fool, sitting around like this," grumbled Yuri. "It's the men who will be seeing all the action."

"It's never foolish to be prepared," Sada told her. Almost to herself, she added, "Part of the trouble is that I haven't been prepared enough. The rebels have taken all the initiative so far."

"Prepared for what?" Yuri asked. "Do you really think they will try to seize the mansion? Why should they?" A bath had removed most of the dirt from her face, but her hands were still grubby.

Sada sighed. "Yuri, you're untidy and undisciplined, but you're not unintelligent. I don't usually have to explain things to you in excessive detail. Now think. If the rebels are not sure that they can get the old lord off the island by boat, what will they try to do next?"

Yuri thought. "So you think they will bring the old lord back here and occupy the mansion?"

"That's what I would do in their place," replied Sada. "This mansion can be defended against attacks for days, even weeks, if the food holds out."

"But what would be the point of the rebels holding out here?" objected Yuri. "Sooner or later our men will be reinforced by others from the mainland, and we can starve them out."

"The mainland," murmured Sada. Here was the real difficulty. Once the news got out that the old lord was at large, would the mainland rally to his support? Perhaps the men in the mainland port town had already swung to the rebels. It had been some time since they had received word from the mainland.

Yuri, as Sada knew, was not slow. "So you think that reinforcements for the rebels might arrive from the port town on the mainland? Does that mean we'll have to stand siege here?"

"Our first task is to get the old lord back in our hands," Sada said, trying to sound encouraging. "While the commander and his men are doing that, we will hold the mansion."

Her face showed only confidence, but in the back of her mind an uneasiness was growing. What had she overlooked? Her husband had gone off with all the fighting men before she had found out what it was that bothering her.

Suddenly she understood it. If the mansion

was so secure, how had the rebels rescued the old lord? How had the ogres managed to get in and slaughter the guards? She refused to believe in the old lord's claims to supernatural natural powers.

"I must see the bodies of the slain guards," she said abruptly.

The sight of the bodies confirmed her suspicious. Three of the men had died of sword wounds, but the fourth man had been stabbed in the back.

The ogres had gained entrance into the mansion because someone had let them in. That same person had also stabbed one of the guards.

There was no time to be lost. "Send me the two maids who waited on the old lord!" Sada ordered. One of the two girls was a traitor. Which one?

The door of the room slid open, and one of the maids, the silent one, entered. She was no longer silent. "You sent for me, my lady?" she asked, smirking.

Then she stepped to one side, and several armed men poured into the room.

Frustrated, Kajiro watched as the boats he wanted fell into the hands of the invaders. He couldn't stop them. They had too many men.

"Why do they want the boats?" asked Matsuzo. Now that the invaders were too busy to attack them, the two men ventured out of the fisherman's cottage to look at the activity on the beach.

Slowly Kajiro and Matsuzo turned and looked at each other. Matsuzo was the first to break the silence. "They must want the boats for taking the old lord off the island. They must have rescued him!"

Kajiro felt himself grow cold with horror. "That means they broke into the mansion and overwhelmed the men in the garrison!"

It was as if mentioning the men in the garrison had conjured them up. Kajiro heard the rush of feet and turned to stare up at the path he had taken earlier. The sinking sun was in his eyes, and all he could see were the black silhouettes of figure after figure pounding down toward the beach.

The rebels, busy with the boats, barely had time to look up before the uniformed soldiers were on them. Some of the rebels were already in boats and were rowing away from the shore. Other boats, in the hands of the soldiers, set off after them.

Matsuzo grinned. "Come on, let's get back into the fight. It's a refreshing change to be on the side with more men for once."

The fight did not last long. Surprised and outnumbered, the rebels fought back fiercely, but were soon overcome. As the prisoners were being tied up by his men, the commander peered at each of the surviving rebels. Finally he shook his head and sighed. "We seem to have misplaced the old lord. Sada will be very cross."

He caught sight of Kajiro and beckoned. "Ah, Zenta. I'm glad to see you. I understand you got here before we did and helped to delay the enemy. Good work!"

"I'm afraid my name isn't really Zenta," began Kajiro, "and I came . . ."

The commander did not seem put off. "That's right: Sada told me you couldn't be Zenta. Well, whoever you are, I'm glad you were here to prevent them from getting all the boats. That reminds me, I'd better make sure that none of the boats got away from us."

The commander, whom Kajiro had always seen slumped in a reverie, was positively bustling as he moved away.

Kajiro wanted to tell the commander that Matsuzo had been the one who had fought the rebels first and had done most of the delaying. He looked around for Matsuzo, and found him talking to a man with a crooked neck.

"This is the boatman who brought me across," Matsuzo told Kajiro. "He has some disturbing new."

The boatman, the same man who had been alarmed by the sight of Kajiro earlier, had taken a long, roundabout route to the mansion. Arriving, he found that the garrison and its commander had already left. He was about to return to the fishing village when he saw something that worried him. The gate of the mansion opened, and a serving girl came out stealthily. After looking around, she called softly, whereupon five men, heavily armed, appeared and slipped through the gate after her.

It looked like treachery. It looked like danger for those left in the mansion.

Chapter 12

"We have to tell the commander right away!" cried Kajiro.

But the commander was no longer on the beach. Fearing that the old lord had been carried away on one of the boats, he and most of his men had taken the remaining boats and had gone off in pursuit. Darkness was setting in, and to delay was to lose sight of the boats entirely. Only four soldiers had been left behind to guard the prisoners.

"I'm going to the mansion," said Kajiro.

"I'll come with you," said Matsuzo. "I wonder if Zenta is at the mansion. Will he be in a condition to fight, in case the rebels break in?"

Kajiro was not thinking of Zenta. His thoughts were on Yuri. What would she think when she found out that he was not a famous warrior, but an imposter? He resolved to fight heroically, to show her that he was more than a seedy ronin, out of condition from drink.

Sada found that she was quite calm. She knew what she had to do: keep these intruders busy until her husband or Gorobei returned.

"What are you doing in my house?" she demanded, glad to find that her voice betrayed no tremor.

The man who had entered first was obviously the leader. He waved to his men to stay back in the hallway, then turned and bowed to Sada. "We merely want to borrow your house for a time," he said politely.

"You look more fetching dressed as a nun," said Yuri. Her voice was also steady. "This man was the one who captured me at the convent," she told Sada. "His specialty is terrorizing nuns and young girls."

Sada recognized him now. He was the "nun" she had met in the scriptures reading hall of the convent. His features, which had seemed so coarse in a nun, were simply the heavy features of a man.

Sada smiled at Yuri. She had never felt so close to her sister. "These brave warriors might be able to overcome a convent of unarmed nuns, but they will find us less easy prey, won't they?"

The rebel leader lost some of his politeness. Clearly he had been unpleasantly surprised to see Yuri, whom he thought he had safely stowed away. His manner became curt. "Lady Sada, I will not waste time. You and your women will be treated with every consideration if you don't try to interfere. We only ask that you stay quietly in this room."

"And allow you to take command of this mansion?" asked Sada. Keep him talking as long as possible, she told herself. "Why do you need our mansion? Don't tell me that you haven't yet taken the old lord off the island? He's still here, isn't he?"

Seeing his scowl, she knew that her words had been on target. "We will gladly receive the old lord here again," she taunted. "We'll even let him have his old room back. Now if you will just go away, everything will be back to normal."

The rebel must have guessed that she was playing for time. "Lady Sada," he said brusquely, "unless you want an undignified struggle, please order your women to surrender their weapons immediately."

"You'll have to take them from us," said Yuri.

She did not speak with her old bravado, but with quiet determination. Sada realized that Yuri's ordeal in the convent had matured her far more effectively than scolding or lecturing from an older sister. For the first time Sada felt more than an exasperated affection for her younger sister. She felt pride.

The rebel leader frowned. Resistance from the women was an irritating obstacle, but he did not expect the delay to last long. "Very well," he grated, advancing into the room with his sword raised.

Uttering a shrill cry, one of Sada's women rushed forward, swinging a halberd. The rebel leader was nearly caught off guard, but not quite. His sword met the shaft of the halberd with a jarring thud as he parried.

The halberd fighter, with a longer reach, can be devastating in battle. But in close combat, a swordsman has greater maneuverability.

One more clash, and the fight was over. The rebel leader barely had time to raise his eyes from the fallen woman before the next one was on him. She was good this second fighter, but she was no match for the swordsman.

Sada's eyes filled with tears when her second fighter fell. This one had been her weapons instructor, and she had learned everything from her.

Even the rebel leader looked shaken. "Tell your women to surrender, Lady Sada," he said huskily. "This massacre is unnecessary."

"We'll never surrender!" said Sada, shaking her head angrily and blinking away her tears. She lifted her halberd and stepped forward.

"No, my lady, let me go first!" cried another of her women, throwing herself between Sada and the rebel.

The rebel swordsman raised his weapon—and stopped. The sound of voices reached them from the direction of the front courtyard. Without removing his eyes from the woman fighter facing him, the rebel slowly backed into the hallway. "Go see what's happening out there," he ordered his men.

The woman halberd fighter wanted to advance, but Sada waved her back. Perhaps her husband's men were returning, or Gorobei. She heard a sudden rush of feet in the hallway, and a clash of weapons. Again her woman warrior wanted to advance, and again Sada waved her back. The hallway was narrow, and entering the fray now might hinder more than help their own side.

Soon most of the clashing seemed to move away to the courtyard. Gripping their weapons, Sada and her women ventured cautiously into the hallway, which was now deserted except for the body of one of the rebels. When they arrived at the courtyard, Sada saw that two men were engaged in fighting the rebels. One was the ronin who had arrived on the island the previous day. The other was a total stranger.

The young stranger was good, Sada could see immediately. He was taking on two of the rebels with no difficulty, and soon one of them fell under his flashing sword.

The ronin, on the other hand, was visibly tiring, although he was acquitting himself much better than Sada had expected. But it was clear that he was no match for the rebel leader, who was a superb swordsman.

Suddenly a blood-curdling squawk pierced the air.

"Raiko!" cried Yuri. "That monster stepped on Raiko's tail!" Swinging her halberd, she dashed forward.

She was no longer needed. The rebel leader, shaken after stepping on Raiko's tail, was unable to parry the ronin's sword.

Only two of the rebels were left. Demoralized by the loss of their leader, they were quickly overcome and disarmed.

Yuri picked up her cat only to find that the injury was mostly to his dignity. The ronin joined her in admiration for Raiko's gallantry. "Let's go and get some more squid for Raiko," he suggested. "Nothing is too good for him."

Sada approached to give her thanks to the young stranger. He bowed gracefully and announced his name. "I am Ishihara Matsuzo."

Sada smiled. "Matsuzo. Yes, I've heard about you. What kept you? We were wondering when you would arrive."

Matsuzo looked up eagerly. "Then Zenta is here? Where is he?"

The convent was deserted. At first the guest moved warily through the silent corridors, walks, and courtyards, keeping his eyes and ears alert for an ambush by one of the conspirators still in the convent. But he encountered no one. He stopped briefly in the kitchen. During the search with Sada and her men, he had noticed that the knives not only had notches on them, but also a sheen of grease. They had been used to cut animal tissue, gristle, and bones. That had confirmed his suspicion that the so-called nuns were not vegetarians. The kitchen was empty, and only a faint smell of the spilled bean paste lingered.

Now he had one more room to search. Holding his sword in his right hand, he slid open the door swiftly with his left hand. Inside there was only one bed with a figure lying on it. It had to be the abbess, the only person with a private sleeping chamber. The abbess lay so still that she appeared lifeless. But when he touched her hand, he could feel warmth. Then he saw the barely perceptible rise and fall of her chest. They must have drugged her, he thought. Carefully he replaced her covers, tucking them around her neck so that she would be kept warm. Later he could try to revive her, but he had other things to do first.

The invaders had gone, most likely down to the harbor. He hoped the commander and his men would be in time to prevent the rebels from seizing all the boats. The question was, had they taken the old lord down to the harbor with them?

If the old lord had been a fully rational man, the answer would be simple: They would just rush him to the harbor and get him aboard a boat as quickly as possible.

But the old man was not rational. If anything unforeseen happened—some clash with the men of the garrison, for example—he might do something quite unpredictable. He might rush into the fight and get himself killed.

The rebels would feel that this was too much of a risk. It would be safer to have the old lord quietly smuggled off the island. There was an obvious place from which they could lower the old man down to a waiting boat—a quiet place, a place the rebels knew well.

Leaving the convent behind him, the guest

directed his steps toward the cliffs. According to the ronin's account, there was a clump of pine trees, and a coil of waiting rope.

He tried to walk slowly, to conserve his strength. The recent loss of blood and fever had weakened him, and he was only just beginning to overcome his giddiness at rising from his sickbed.

The sun had set when he saw the pine trees at the edge of the cliff, as described by the ronin. In the evening light the sky was a deep pink, and the thin branches and needles of the pine trees seemed to be painted in black ink with the tip of a brush.

He stopped. Two figures were standing by the trees, and he could hear voices.

"No, no, no, no!" said the querulous voice of an old man. "Where did all the ogres go? They came for me, and I want to wait for them!"

"Yes, the ogres did come for you, my lord," said his companion soothingly. "But now that you are free, you no longer need them. They have gone."

"I want them!" insisted the old man. "I won't move until the ogres come back!"

The guest approached quietly. He had long ago perfected the art of moving without sound. The scene gave him a grim satisfaction. The rebels had used the old man's delusion about ogres to spread terror in the garrison. But now this same delusion was making him balky.

"Ogres of the island, I command you to

appear!" cried the old man, raising his voice.

His companion turned away and bent down to fumble with something in a pack. When he straightened, his head had changed shape and was covered by a shock of light-colored hair. Two horns sprang from the top of his head.

"Ah," said the old man. "Greetings! I'm glad that you've come back."

"I've returned at your command, my lord," said the transformed man. Even his voice was changed and sounded more hollow. "Will you allow me to bring you off the island? We are going by boat to a place where there are many more of my kind."

"But why aren't there more of you now?" complained the old man. "I saw four of you earlier." He looked around.

The senses of the mad are sometimes more acute than those of the sane. The old man pointed at the new arrival. "Here comes another one of you!" Then his face fell. "No, it's just another human being."

The horned figure whirled about. Seen in full face, its countenance was a shock. The huge, bulging eyes and creased brows were fixed in sorrow, while the grinning, fanged mouth was fixed in glee. This conflict increased the eeriness of his face.

A hollow voice issued from the rigidly set mouth. "What do you hope to do here?"

The guest approached slowly. "I hope to convince his lordship to wait," he said. He bowed to the old man. "Descending these cliffs by rope is unsafe, my lord. Why not wait until more of your ogres appear with a litter, and then you can travel with them in comfort."

"He's going down now!" said the hollow voice. "More of the ogres are waiting for him below."

Carefully watching the horned figure from the corner of his eye, the guest kept his face turned respectfully toward the old man. "My lord, you must not permit him to tie a rope around your waist and lower you like a sack of rice. It's an insult to your dignity, an insult to your high status as a daimyo."

In the monstrous face of his adversary, the eyes continued to sorrow and the mouth continued to rejoice, but the horned head was vibrating with fury. "And I say that he must go down these cliffs now! You can't stop me!"

"I can, and I will," the guest said flatly.

There was a long silence. Then a hiss escaped the fanged mouth. "Now I see! *You* are Konishi Zenta! I should have guessed. We heard that you were in the province, and that Lady Sada had sent for you. That's why we delayed our operation—we hoped to recruit you to our side. If we had known that you were incapacitated, we wouldn't have waited!"

Zenta, who was Lady Sada's guest, nodded. "That was the reason why Lady Sada tried to keep my identity a secret. If the men at the garrison had known that she had sent for help, and that the helper was useless, their morale would have suffered."

A hollow chuckle sounded from the grinning, gaping mouth. "I was relieved when that poor, alcoholic ronin arrived and announced that he was Zenta. But I'm even more relieved that it turns out to be *you*. He at least has no trouble staying on his feet."

Zenta knew that he had one chance only to win this engagement. His opponent had every advantage, except . . .

He flashed a glance up at the sky, and instinctively his opponent followed his gaze. Speed had always been Zenta's greatest asset. His sword flashed out an instant before his opponent's.

He felt his sword making contact, but the action had taken all his remaining strength, and for a moment he could not even lift his head to watch for his opponent's riposte. But his opponent did not move. Finally Zenta found the strength to turn and look.

The horned head had not changed its expression, but from the grinning mouth a thin trickle of blood was flowing. The trickle changed to a gush. Still clutching his sword, the figure crashed to the ground.

Hearing a whimpering behind him, Zenta turned to the old lord. Tears were pouring down the old man's face. "You've killed my ogre!" he sobbed. "You've killed my friend!"

"He's not a real ogre," Zenta said quickly.

"He was only pretending. Look, he was wearing an ogre mask."

Bending down, he unhooked the mask from the dead face. It was the mask that had given him the slimmest possible edge, the edge he needed to win the fight. When both men raised their faces, inertia caused the mask to slip, so that for an instant—an instant no longer than a split second—the masked man's eyes were covered. That was what Zenta had been counting on.

Zenta held up the mask and showed it to the old lord. It was an unusually beautiful piece of folk art, made by the local farmers for their village festivals.

He did not anticipate the result of his action. The old lord began to scream. "You killed my ogre! You cut off his head!"

Zenta hurried to calm the frenzied old man. "This is not a head! Look! It's only a mask!"

But Zenta's approach only drove the old man into a greater panic. Step by step he retreated. "No, no, don't touch me!"

Suddenly he tottered, and his arms flailed. Zenta threw himself at the edge of the cliff and grabbed frantically at a sleeve. But the old man was already falling. The cloth tore from Zenta's fingers.

He heard one last scream, and then silence. Finally he crawled over to the edge and looked down at the base of the cliff, at the pathetic bundle lying unmoving on the rocks below. It was his fault. He had not been strong enough to hold on.

Above the sound of the crashing waves he heard a wailing. It was too close to be a sea gull. He saw black figures gathering around the body of the old lord. The nuns from the grotto were weeping.

Chapter 13

Kajiro saw Matsuzo talking to Lady Sada. They were smiling. Then he heard Matsuzo mention Zenta's name, and they both burst out laughing. He could guess what they were laughing at: his clumsy impersonation of Zenta.

"We need more squid for Raiko," said Yuri's voice. She was looking up at him, and in her eyes he saw gratitude, respect, and friendship. How her expression would change when she found out he was an imposter! With Matsuzo's arrival, she would find out momentarily. He didn't want to be there when that happened.

"You can get the squid," he muttered. "I want to go and arrange a rescue for those nuns in the grotto." Without waiting for her reply, he hurried away.

Reaching the gate, he heard quick steps following him. Was Yuri coming after him? Half relieved, half disappointed, he saw that it was Matsuzo.

"Lady Sada said that Zenta has gone to the convent," said the young samurai. "I want to go and see what he is doing. Do you want to come along?"

Facing Zenta, the man he had impersonated, was not something Kajiro looked forward to doing. He was about to make his excuses when

Matsuzo said, "Zenta wouldn't have gone to the convent if he hadn't expected some trouble there. He may need us. I'd be glad if you can help me." His manner held no trace of condescension, and his request for help sounded sincere.

"All right," said Kajiro gruffly. He took a deep breath. "I can show you the way. In fact, since coming to the island, I've done nothing but run back and forth between the mansion, the convent, the cliffs, and the harbor. I could probably make the circuit in my sleep tonight."

Reaching the convent, the two men found the gate standing open. They made a rapid search of the compound. They found no one except the abbess, lying in a deep, drugged sleep. Awake she was an awesome figure, but asleep she looked pathetic. He remembered catching a flicker of fear in her eyes, and now he knew he had not imagined it. Her convent had been overrun by armed rebels, who were holding her and the other nuns as prisoners. A false move on her part could have brought death to the nuns in the grotto.

"She seems to be unharmed," observed Matsuzo. "Shall we try to wake her?"

Kajiro was more comfortable with the abbess asleep than with her awake. "As long as she is unharmed, we should just let her sleep off the drug. Anyway, it's better to let her own nuns take care of her. Our job is to get them out of the grotto and bring them back to the convent."

"I wonder where Zenta could have gone," said Matsuzo, looking worried.

Kajiro knew the answer immediately. "To the cliffs. That's where he must have gone."

He was right. The last of the daylight was nearly gone when they reached the cliffs. There was just enough light to show a man seated with his back against a pine tree.

Matsuzo began to run. At their approach the man raised his head. It was Lady Sada's guest. On seeing Matsuzo he smiled. "Well, so you finally arrived."

Matsuzo grinned, and then his face sobered. "You don't look terribly well," he told Zenta. "Should you be up?"

"Probably not," said Zenta. "Actually, I'm tired—and disgusted with myself."

Kajiro started. He saw a body stretched out on the ground, one hand still clutching a sword. I see that you've had a fight."

"Did he . . ." Matsuzo began.

"He didn't touch me," said Zenta. "Don't worry, I'm really in better shape than I look."

Kajiro peered at the dead man's face and received a shock. "It's Gorobei!"

"Yes," said Zenta heavily. "I should have known we had a traitor right in the mansion. I can't understand why I didn't guess earlier. That fever must have affected my brains."

"But you couldn't have known it was Gorobei," said Kajiro, still shaken by the discovery. "He was such a good officer. Lady Sada trusted him completely." And Yuri would mourn for him, he added to himself

"Now that I know, I can see that everything pointed to Gorobei," said Zenta. "He grew up on the island, and he would have known about the grotto, most likely. Also, the traitor had to be someone with authority. Gorobei had the best opportunity to visit the old lord secretly. He could tell his men to wait outside while he searched the room. Alone with the old lord, he could wear his ogre mask."

Zenta paused. "The old lord mentioned seeing a tall ogre and a short one. If Gorobei was the tall ogre, who was the short one? Did we have not one, but two traitors in the mansion?"

"Yes, there were two traitors," said Kajiro. "And I know who must have been the short ogre. It was the girl—you weren't there when Lady Sada discovered that one of the maids serving the old lord was working for the rebels."

"It seems to me that we've had carelessness all around," said Matsuzo wryly.

"I'm afraid there's worse to come," said Zenta. "Look below."

He pointed, and Kajiro and Matsuzo went to the edge of the cliff. Looking down, they saw some huddled shapes, and realized they were the nuns gathering around something lying on the rocks.

"Who . . . who is it?" asked Matsuzo.

"The former daimyo," Zenta said bitterly.

All that plotting, fighting, and killing had

been for nothing. The rebels had lost their fig-
urehead, and the garrison their prisoner.

"Did he kill himself?" asked Kajiro finally.

Zenta sighed. "It's impossible to say what he
intended, or didn't intend. But between us,
Gorobei and I drove him to his death. He was
crazed with terror, and he kept on retreating
toward the cliff until he fell."

Something glittering on the ground caught
Kajiro's eye. It looked like a pair of golden
horns. It *was* a pair of golden horns. He went
over and found himself looking at the reverse
side of a mask. Turning it over, he saw the
round, staring eyes and grinning fanged mouth
of an ogre mask.

"I might have known!" he said disgustedly.
"This was made by the local farmers, wasn't it?"

Zenta nodded. "When you described the
strange behavior of the farmers, I guessed they
had been terrorized by the invaders, who must
have forced them to hand over their festival
masks."

"And I thought the farmers were in terror
because they really believed in the ogres,"
admitted Kajiro. He felt very foolish. "I thought
they were trying to appease the ogres by sacrificing their animals."

"Then what did happen to the animals?"
asked Matsuzo.

"Remember that this is a small island, with
a very limited supply of food," said Zenta.
"When the invaders arrived, the population

195

here rose sharply. They had to feed some thirty to forty more mouths."

"I see," said Matsuzo slowly. "The animals were butchered for meat!"

Kajiro suddenly remembered the slobbering sound he had heard in one of the farm sheds. "I think one of the rebels was so starved that he started to eat some of the meat raw."

Matsuzo looked revolted. "Eat raw meat? You mean raw chicken meat?"

"Why not?" said Zenta. "You love raw fish."

"Yes, but raw fish is different!" protested Matsuzo.

"Remember those Europeans we met in Miyako?" said Zenta. "They told me that some people even *prefer* their meat to be bloody."

"Europeans probably have different digestive systems," said Matsuzo. "Wait! Wasn't there some talk here of dogs disappearing too?"

"I think they took the watchdogs to prevent them from giving the alarm while the chickens were being stolen," said Zenta. "They may not have eaten the dogs, although if you're hungry enough, dog meat would be as good as any other red meat."

Matsuzo still looked sickened. "But to eat raw meat, with blood running down their chins!"

"They didn't always have to eat the meat raw," said Zenta. "At the convent kitchen, I saw evidence that someone had been cutting up meat. They could well have cooked it there."

"You guessed, didn't you, that the so-called

nuns were eating meat," said Matsuzo. "When did you first suspect?"

"Raiko gave me the first clue," replied Zenta. He turned to Kajiro. "When you told me about Raiko's behavior in the kitchen, I wondered whether it wasn't because he had been excited by the smell of blood. The 'nuns' tried to cover up the smell of their butchering by spilling pickles, but Raiko's nose was too good for them."

Kajiro remembered Raiko's excitement at finding the bloodstained area near the cliffs. "I suppose they disposed of the bones of the dogs and chickens by throwing them into the whirlpool. Gorobei must have been worried that I might see traces of the butchering. That's why he kicked over Raiko's basket. He thought we'd be too busy chasing the cat to search the ground thoroughly. In fact, his plan backfired, since Raiko led us straight to the bloodstains."

Zenta smiled grimly. "Gorobei had too many things on his hands. He had to lead the searchers away from possible clues, and he also had to worry about feeding an increasing number of hungry rebels in hiding."

Kajiro nodded. "They are muscular fighting men, and needed a lot of nourishing food."

"They would certainly want to eat more heartily than the nuns," said Matsuzo, convinced at last. "You could tell from their build that they were men in disguise?" he asked Zenta.

"It was not that," said Zenta. "They enveloped

197

themselves in loose robes, and they were probably hunched over to disguise their height. But men walk differently from women. They tried to take small mincing steps, but we managed to provoke them into forgetting themselves at one point. But what I noticed first was their teeth."

Kajiro remembered the big, shining teeth. "I see what you mean. Nuns who live on a diet of rice and pickles don't have teeth like that."

Zenta began to question Matsuzo about his recent adventures. Listening to the younger man describe his captivity and escape, Kajiro felt left out. He bowed and said that he wanted to return to the mansion and arrange a rescue for the nuns. Zenta nodded, and went back to listening to Matsuzo's account.

He had made himself a perfect fool over the missing animals, Kajiro thought, as he walked away. His theory about the farmers sacrificing to the ogres was ridiculous, the product of a wine-sodden mind. Zenta, who had had less opportunity to investigate, had arrived at the truth.

Nor was Kajiro proud of his fighting ability. He hadn't done too badly at the harbor, although he had some help from the fishermen and their floats. But he would never have stood up to a swordsman like Gorobei. Zenta, hardly up from his sickbed, had killed Gorobei with a single swordstroke. The very thought of his attempted impersonation made him writhe with embarrassment.

Kajiro would have been very surprised by the conversation taking place back at the cliffs between Zenta and Matsuzo.

"Look, Kajiro has gone to get help for those poor nuns," said Zenta, "while we just sit here talking idly."

"He seems like a thoroughly decent man," said Matsuzo.

"I wonder what he's doing on the island, though," said Zenta.

"Looking for work, I imagine," said Matsuzo.

Zenta still looked doubtful. "Yes, but why on the island? He would have a much better chance of finding work on the mainland."

"Anyway, he fought well at the harbor," said Matsuzo. "I was nearly finished when he arrived. If he could just stay away from drink, he would do very well."

"He has already done very well," said Zenta. "He's the one who discovered the grotto and rescued the girl Yuri. In fact the false Zenta seems to have done better than the real one. All I did was get the old lord killed."

"It wasn't entirely your fault," said Matsuzo quickly. "Everyone has made mistakes here. The commander allowed the invaders to land secretly on the island, and Lady Sada let one of her serving women betray her."

"Lady Sada asked me to help, and I failed her," said Zenta. "When the young daimyo asks who is responsible for the death of his father, I shall have to answer for it."

Chapter 14

The whole garrison was at the harbor, watching the flotilla from the mainland approach. The morning sun was in their eyes, and the boats were black spots dancing on the waves. At least twenty boats were approaching, each one filled with armed men. Resistance was useless.

Sada and her husband were seated on stools unfolded for them on the beach. The rest of the men stood at attention. Behind them were poles set upright in the sand and hung with black-and-white striped canvas, creating almost a stage for the assembled company. If they had to surrender, they might as well surrender in style, thought Sada.

She glanced at her husband, who sat with his usual abstracted air. For the first time she realized that his eyes, so vacant-looking, actually saw more than she had expected. "You had already suspected Gorobei, hadn't you?" she asked softly.

"I knew he was dangerously ambitious," he replied. "I also thought he might resent our authority here. After all, his family commanded the island at one time, and he probably thought the command here should have gone to him. When the young daimyo appointed your father, Gorobei must have been very bitter."

Her husband, despite his absentmindedness, had seen Gorobei more clearly than she had. And she was so proud of her judgment! "If you suspected Gorobei of treachery, why didn't you tell me?" she asked. "Then we might have avoided all this!"

"I was afraid you wouldn't believe me," he said simply. "I was afraid you would think that I was accusing Gorobei out of jealousy."

She was angry, more with herself than with him, because there was some truth in what he said. "Ridiculous!" she muttered. "Why should I think that?"

He continued to look into space. "I knew Gorobei was interested in you at first, and only turned his attention to Yuri when your father arranged your marriage to me. But what I didn't know were *your* feelings about the marriage—or about Gorobei."

"I respected Gorobei's abilities as an officer," she said gruffly. "But I was never fond of him, if that's what you mean."

"I know that now," said her husband, carefully looking at no one. After a moment, he said, "I wanted you to think well of me, and that's why I was afraid to speak out. Because of that, I've failed in my duty." He pulled out a flat metal box from his sash. Opening the box, he took out a brush and a small bottle of ink.

"What are you doing?" she asked.

"I'm working on my death poem," he said.

He had started the poem on the previous day,

and she had not taken him seriously. Now she bit her lip and said nothing.

Zenta moved forward. He had seen the ink bottle and brush. "A death poem may not be necessary, sir," he told the commander. He peered at the nearest boat, which was close enough for them to see the uniform clothing of the men inside. "These men may not be rebels. They may have been sent by the daimyo."

"Whether they are rebels or the daimyo's men, I'm finished," said the commander. "Through my neglect, the old lord is dead, and since I'm in charge here, the blame is entirely mine."

"Hardly, sir," said Zenta. "*I* was the one who allowed the old lord to fall to his death."

Sada broke in. "Let's not speak of that until we see who the men are." She had her own plans for placing the blame.

The first boat landed, followed almost immediately by several others. Already the first of the landing party was moving up the beach.

The commander gasped. "It's the daimyo's chamberlain himself!"

The man he indicated walked slowly to the reception party in front of the canvas. He was a middle-aged man, slender and not especially tall, but carrying himself very straight. Sada had never met the chamberlain, but had heard her father describe him as a hard man, and deeply cunning. If he threw his support to the rebels, the young daimyo's cause was lost.

Whichever side the chamberlain was on,

there was nothing the island garrison could do now except bow to authority. Sada and her husband rose from their stools and sank to their knees, as did everyone else in the reception party.

The chamberlain's first words made his position clear. "We received news that the rebels are trying to invade this island in the name of the former daimyo," he said, his voice unexpectedly deep for such a slight man. "I see that we may not be needed here. You seem to have things under control."

The commander raised his eyes. "Yes, your lordship, the invaders have been defeated and captured."

"Very good!" said the chamberlain. "The daimyo will be very pleased by your vigilance."

There was a slight pause. Then the commander cleared his throat. "The conspiracy on the mainland has not been widespread, then?"

The chamberlain looked displeased at the question. Perhaps he felt that affairs on the mainland were not the concern of the island commander. But he consented to answer the question. "No, the conspiracy was confined to the port town on the mainland across from this island. The plotters were arrested, largely due to the alertness and courage of an inn servant in the town."

"It must be Kimi!" said a voice. Sada turned, and saw that the speaker was Matsuzo. He blushed and bowed his head again.

The chamberlain, however, smiled at the young samurai. "Yes, the name of that servant girl was Kimi. And you must be the young gentleman she helped to escape. I see that you arrived here in time to give warning."

"The conspirators on the mainland have been arrested," continued the chamberlain. "They attempted to subvert my officers in the port town, but the men stayed true."

"Excuse me," said Matsuzo again, "but one of the conspirators, a man with very close-set eyes, was away from the inn at the time of my escape. I think he must be a leader in the rebellion."

"He has been captured," said the chamberlain. "He was in fact the instigator of the whole plot, a man of high rank at the daimyo's court, and of high esteem—especially self-esteem."

The grim note in the chamberlain's voice told his listeners that there would be no mercy for the conspirators. Sada could not suppress a shudder. They were working to further their own ambitions, the conspirators, but it could also be argued that they were loyal samurai, being true to the old lord to whom they had sworn undying faith.

The chamberlain waved his hand and indicated that all the company could rise. "Let us go to your mansion. I must see the old lord briefly, so that I can report to my master, who is anxious about the health of his father."

No one moved. The commander, Sada, and

all their company stayed kneeling on the ground.

The chamberlain stared at them in chilly surprise. Finally the commander spoke. "My lord, a most tragic thing has happened. Because of the fighting and the turmoil, there was considerable confusion . . ." His voice trailed to a stop.

"What are you trying to tell me?" asked the chamberlain. His voice was dangerously quiet.

The commander swallowed, and then his words came out in a rush. "The old lord is dead."

It was silent on the beach, except for the flapping of the canvas in the breeze. From a distance came the raucous cry of a sea gull.

"I see," said the chamberlain finally. His face was completely expressionless. "Can you tell me what happened?"

While the commander struggled for words, Sada spoke up. "My lord, please pardon a mere woman for speaking. My husband is too overcome to speak coherently."

The chamberlain's eyes narrowed. "Very well, lady, you may speak."

Sada's heart was pounding. If she made a mistake, a number of people, people she cared deeply about, could lose their lives. "My lord," she began, "the safety of the old lord was entrusted to our most able officer, Gorobei."

"I know Gorobei's family," said the chamberlain. "They are well-connected and well regarded by the daimyo. Go on."

The next part was the most delicate. "When news of the rebel attack came," Sada continued, "we decided that keeping the harbor in our hands was the most important. So long as we controlled the boats, no one could leave the island."

The chamberlain nodded agreement. Encour- aged, Sada went on. "We therefore sent the greater part of our men to the harbor, leaving Gorobei and a small force behind to guard the old lord."

By now, the men of the garrison must know that she was lying. But it was in their interest to keep quiet. "What happened next is my fault, entirely," she said, and paused.

She had the chamberlain's total attention now. "Yes, yes, go on," he said impatiently.

"My lord," said Sada, "the selection of the serving women in the mansion is wholly my responsibility, and it was through my careless- ness that one of the women turned out to be a traitor."

"It was inexcusable carelessness!" said the chamberlain.

"I make no excuses," said Sada. Then she added softly, "Yet identifying traitors is not always an easy task."

She did not have to say more. Almost echo- ing in the air were the chamberlain's own words, spoken only moments earlier: a high-ranking member of the daimyo's court had been plotting undetected for weeks on the mainland.

"Very well," said the chamberlain. "Go on."

Was he actually hiding a smile? Sada began to hope. "The treacherous serving girl unlocked the gate and admitted a party of rebels. Gorobei and his men fought valiantly, but they were cut down, every one. I lost two of my bravest women warriors, who formed the last defense. But the worst was that the old lord was driven frantic during the fighting, and rushed out of the mansion toward the cliffs. We ran after him and tried to reassure him, but he was too distracted to listen. Before we could overtake him, he fell or threw himself over the edge. We found his body on the rocks below, and it is now resting in the mansion."

She knew her story had a number of weaknesses. It was hard enough for the old man to walk unaided to the cliff. For him to outrun his pursuers was all but unbelievable.

But the chamberlain said nothing and remained thoughtful. Sada stole a look at his face and said, "My lord, if you must place the blame on someone, place it on Gorobei and on me. He paid with his life, and I am fully prepared to pay with mine."

At last the chamberlain spoke. "Lady, that will not be necessary. I will bring the news of Gorobei's death to his family, and they will be glad to know that he died so heroically." He sighed deeply. "The old lord is dead, and there is nothing we can do to change that sad fact." He gave a signal to his men. "Now, let us go to the mansion. I must arrange for the conveyance of his body to the mainland."

This time Sada was certain that the chamberlain was hiding a smile. Whether he believed her story or not, he was accepting it officially. She had a shrewd idea why.

At the funeral feast, the chamberlain confirmed Sada's suspicions. The meal was makeshift, for it was not easy to serve more than a hundred unexpected guests. Since the dinner was merely a token gesture, however, to mark their respect for the former daimyo, all that was needed was a mouthful of rice for each person with a small dish of pickled vegetables. Taking out all their reserves of wine, Sada and her women were able to pour each man at least one small cup. She personally poured for the chamberlain, while Yuri saw to his chief officers.

The chamberlain did not try to hide his good humor. Sada saw him lean over and speak confidentially to her husband. "Regrettable as it is, the death of the old lord is not necessarily a total disaster."

The commander bowed his head, but his thoughts seemed to be far away. It was not certain that he understood or even heard his guest.

The chamberlain went on. "As long as the old lord was alive, subversive elements within the province would always use him as a rallying point for revolt. They much prefer a puppet as their leader to a dynamic young daimyo, who keeps a sharp eye on the affairs of his domain."

He smiled at Sada as she leaned down to refill his wine cup. "Lady, I knew your father, and I always had the utmost respect for his abilities. Your gallant defense of the island is no shame to his memory."

Turning back to the commander, the chamberlain dropped his voice nearly to a whisper. "Naturally the daimyo will be deeply grieved by his father's death, but there are people who will see it as an act of providence. You need not fear censure for your conduct in affair. I will see to it that your men are rewarded for their bravery."

Sada kept her face impassive, but felt relief wash over her. Although she had guessed that this would be the chamberlain's attitude, she wanted the assurance of hearing him express it aloud.

Kajiro left soon after the brief meal was finished. The chamberlain, now in a very good humor, lingered in the dining hall to talk to the commander, while his men waited patiently in the courtyard for his orders. Kajiro felt no desire to join the waiting men.

He had to think about his future. The temptation was great to have one more talk with Yuri. He didn't want to leave the island without telling her that his impersonation of Zenta had been accidental and unplanned. But she was busy helping her sister with the guests. Besides, she was probably still grieving for Gorobei, and would be too unhappy to talk to him.

At least he had derived some good from his island sojourn. His reflexes had improved more than he had thought possible, and he could run some distance without getting out of breath. Best of all, his desire for wine had almost disappeared. At dinner, he had had only one small cup of wine, but he had been able to look without envy at the chamberlain, who was having his cup refilled. Since coming to the island, Kajiro had been simply too busy to drink. Perhaps his drinking had started because of his loneliness and idleness.

But as he trudged toward the fishing village, he was lonely again. For a while, he had a sense of camaraderie with Matsuzo, with Yuri, even with Raiko. Now he was alone again, and he had to make a decision about where he would spend the night, and the next night.

At least he would visit the fisherman family and say good-bye to them. They had been the first to welcome him to the island, and they had supplied him with pieces of dried squid for Raiko. Even after they had learned that he was not Zenta, they had continued to be friendly.

On reaching the harbor, he was glad to see that the fisherman's cottage had been repaired after the damage sustained during the rebel attack on the village. Since it was a simple construction of wooden boards, repairs were also simple.

The two young boys saw him first as he approached the house. They looked shyly at him, and then turned and ran into the house calling for their father. The fisherman came out and greeted Kajiro with a welcoming smile. "Ah, I see you've come for more dried squid. My wife has a nice big one all ready for you."

"No, that's not why I came today," began Kajiro. He stopped, feeling a bump against the back of his leg. Raiko was squinting up at him with yellow eyes, and he began to purr ingratiatingly. The cat had evidently followed him all the way from the mansion.

Kajiro pointed sternly back toward the mansion. "Shoo!" Go back! Go home!"

His gesture lost its effectiveness when the fisherman's wife put a large dried squid in his hand. He found himself waving the squid at Raiko, as if inviting the cat to help himself.

The two little boys laughed with delight, and soon Kajiro laughed with them. He tore off a strip of the squid for Raiko, and sat down with the boys to watch the cat eat.

The fisherman's wife invited Kajiro into the house for tea. "It's not very good tea, so I've added some toasted rice for flavor," she apologized.

More than the tea, Kajiro welcomed her friendliness. It would be hard to leave these people, to leave this island.

The fisherman already knew about the death of the former daimyo. "Our young lord won't have to worry so much about rebellion now," he said with satisfaction.

Kajiro learned that most of the fishermen, both on the island and on the mainland, had been happy when the young daimyo took power. During the reign of the old lord, corruption had been widespread, and the fishermen regularly lost the best part of their catches as bribery to the tax collectors.

"We are grateful to you, sir, for the part you took in putting down the rebellion," said the fisherman, suddenly turning formal and bowing.

Kajiro was embarrassed. "Don't thank me," he mumbled. "I didn't really do much."

"Yes, you did, you rescued Raiko," said a voice. It was Yuri, holding Raiko in her arms.

Raiko jumped out of her arms and landed heavily next to Kajiro. Confused, not knowing where to look, the ronin bent to stroke the cat. "Raiko rescued me more often than I did him," he said. "He nearly sacrificed his tail during the fight in the mansion when I was getting the worst of it."

Yuri entered the house and sat down, accepting a cup of tea brought over hurriedly by the fisherman's wife. "Why did you leave so suddenly?" she asked. "The commander was telling the chamberlain about how you discovered the grotto, and we couldn't find you.

Then when I saw that Raiko was gone, I guessed that you'd both be here."

The fisherman's wife left the room, pulling her two sons after her, and quietly closed the door.

Kajiro continued to stroke Raiko, who purred so hard that his whole body seemed to vibrate. "You were all busy talking," he said. "So I thought I might as well leave."

"I wasn't busy at all," said Yuri. "We finished with the food and wine quite soon, since there was hardly anything to serve."

"Well, I didn't see any reason to stay," mumbled Kajiro.

After a moment, Yuri gave Kajiro a sidelong glance. "There *was* a reason for you to stay," she said softly. "I wanted to thank you for saving me from the grotto."

Kajiro's heart began to beat a little faster. "I didn't want to bother you, knowing you must be grieving for Gorobei."

"Gorobei!" cried Yuri. "What makes you think I'd grieve for *him*?"

Kajiro stared at her in wonder. "But you and Gorobei were always scrapping and exchanging insults. I could tell that you were interested in each other."

Yuri gave an unladylike snort. "You must be used to a strange sort of girl if you think that insulting a man shows she's interested in him!"

"At least I know that Gorobei was interested in *you*," said Kajiro. He felt breathless. "And

213

since he was a handsome young samurai from a distinguished family, I naturally thought you'd be glad of his attention."

"He was ambitious," retorted Yuri. "By now you must know that he was a very ambitious man. He wanted to marry Sada at first, and when she married someone else, he turned his attention, as you call it, to me." Again she stole a glance at him, and then quickly dropped her eyes. "Couldn't you tell the difference between the way I felt about you and about Gorobei?"

Hope rose almost painfully in Kajiro. "I thought you were friendly to me because you took me for Zenta," he said. "And I was afraid you'd despise me once you found out that I was only an imposter."

For once Yuri's manner held no trace of her usual teasing willfulness. "You were not an imposter. When people thought you were Zenta, you *became* Zenta. You were brave because you were expected to be brave. Do you know why I was so childish sometimes? People treated me like a child—Sada, my father, Gorobei—especially Gorobei. So I acted the way they expected me to."

"But I don't think you're a child at all!" said Kajiro.

"I know," said Yuri, and her voice was husky. "You're different from all the rest of them."

Kajiro wanted to reach out for her, but his hands encountered Raiko, who began to lick his fingers.

Yuri snatched up her cat and buried her face in his fur. "If you leave me, who's going to help me look for Raiko next time he runs away?"

Sada was relieved when the chamberlain finally announced his departure. Her hospitality had been stretched to the limit, and unless they obtained food from the mainland soon, the whole garrison would be living on seaweed soup.

"I know it's unseemly to cut short the funeral feast and hurry away," apologized the chamberlain. "But if I delayed, news of the old lord's death might reach the ears of the young daimyo. Who knows what sort of wild rumor he might hear." His eyes twinkled. "I'm sure you will understand that I must reach the castle first with my own account of the tragedy."

Sada and the commander hastened to express their agreement and their gratitude. The chamberlain's eyes went to the courtyard. "That's Konishi Zenta over there, isn't it? One of your men pointed him out to me. Tell him I wish to speak to him."

Sada sent a serving woman with the chamberlain's request. Zenta made his way through the crowded room and over to the chamberlain. He bowed, murmuring his name.

The chamberlain smiled graciously. "The commander was fortunate in having you here to help him repel the invaders."

Zenta shook his head. "Actually, I didn't lift

a finger. Because of an indisposition, I was a passive observer in this whole affair."

Sada knew that he was struggling to suppress a smile. To describe his role completely would include mentioning his part in the death of the old lord. Nor would it be tactful to tell the chamberlain that he had slain Gorobei, now universally hailed as a hero.

"I'm sure you're being too modest," said the chamberlain. "I understand that you are unattached to any lord at the moment. I'm prepared to offer you a position in our clan."

Zenta bowed politely and murmured that he was still convalescent, and would be unable to commit himself. Recognizing reluctance, the chamberlain did not press further.

"However, my lord," said Zenta, "if there is space in one of your boats, may my friend and I beg a ride back to the mainland?"

As he spoke, his eyes met Sada's, and she knew he was silently saying farewell. For an instant her heart clenched painfully. Then she turned her head away.

"Certainly," said the chamberlain. "I'm sure we can find room." His eyes went to the gate. It was just opening to admit Kajiro and Yuri, both of them looking slightly flushed. "I should also like to offer a job to that ronin, Kajiro, whose valiant actions helped defeat the rebels."

The commander was observing the couple. "I suspect that Kajiro will be settling on the island, my lord."

"Permit me, at least, to make him an offer," said the chamberlain.

The chamberlain faced Kajiro alone in the study. "Well, what have you found out?"

"The only thing I have to report is that the commander is completely loyal to the regime of the daimyo," said Kajiro. "You have no reason to suspect him of treachery."

"But can anyone really be as vacant as all that?" asked the chamberlain doubtfully. "I just can't believe that the man is such an empty-headed fool."

Kajiro remembered enduring the commander's sharp gaze while discussing the matter of Yuri—and in fact the interview had taken place in this very room. "The commander may look like a dreamer, my lord, but he is no fool. His eyes are sharp enough. I'm positive he is no traitor, however. I think the recent events here should prove that."

"Very well," said the chamberlain. "I'll take your word for it." He took a small package from his sleeve. "Here is your pay. Are you coming back with us to the mainland?"

Kajiro made no move to take the money. "No, my lord. I'm no longer in your service. In fact I realize that I must have left your service two days ago."

The chamberlain raised his brows. "Well, well . . ." He smiled. "The word is that you fought well here on the island. I'm prepared to offer you permanent employment."

As Kajiro shook his head and began to speak, the chamberlain added, "No longer as a secret spy, but as a regular samurai in service at the castle."

Four days earlier, Kajiro would have been elated by the offer. It was everything he had looked for during all these long months of unemployment. But now he only shook his head again. "I'm grateful for the offer, my lord, but I intend to stay on the island."

On the way down to the harbor with the chamberlain's men, Matsuzo looked curiously at Zenta. "If you're feeling so poorly, why don't you stay on the island for a bit?"

"I don't want to cause the people here any more inconvenience," Zenta said shortly. "They have enough to do on the island."

Zenta's face was stony. Matsuzo suddenly remembered the spasm of pain on Lady Sada's face when she heard Zenta say he was leaving. He also knew that Zenta, for his part, admired her. He was strongly attracted to women with wit and courage, and Lady Sada had both. But Zenta was fearful of forming deep attachments, as a result of an early family tragedy. It afflicted him with an acute restlessness that drove him from place to place. Perhaps one day he would meet someone who could cure him of the restlessness. Meanwhile, anyone who wished to remain his friend had to endure this life of ceaseless wandering.

Matsuzo wasn't altogether sorry that they were leaving. "The commander was showing me some of his poems last night. To tell the truth, they were dreadful, and I had trouble finding something nice to say about them. But I finally managed a few polite words. And then he wanted to bring out all his old poems to show me!" An indefatigable poet himself, Matsuzo was a pitiless critic of mediocre work.

"We can't always be objective about our own work," remarked Zenta. Why did he seem to be biting his lips on a smile? At least his mood was brightening.

"I know what we can do," suggested Matsuzo. "We can go back to Kimi's inn. I want to thank her for helping me escape. Besides, the food they served there was delicious, although I wasn't enjoying it much at the time."

"A good dinner is just what we need," agreed Zenta. "And that's another reason for leaving the island. They're short of food, and I don't want to be here when they start serving dog meat!"

Down by the boats they saw Kajiro. He looked acutely uncomfortable. "I came to say how sorry I am for my impersonation of you," he told Zenta. "I needed to stay on the island because . . ."

"You don't have to say any more," Zenta interrupted quickly. "Besides, your impersonation didn't do my reputation any harm. On the contrary, considering how miserably I did on the island, I wish you had kept up the impersonation a little longer!"

"Are you leaving the island as well?" Matsuzo asked Kajiro. "If you are, we'd welcome your company."

"I'm honored," said Kajiro, and he was sincere. "But I will be staying on."

Matsuzo suddenly remembered seeing Kajiro and Yuri returning to the mansion together. "Lady Yuri would have no objection to the idea."

Kajiro blushed. "We have an understanding, the two of us. But we'll have to wait and see how the commander and Lady Sada feel about it."

"You won't have to worry about that," said Matsuzo. "I heard how the commander praised you to the chamberlain in the dining hall."

Kajiro's blush deepened. "I didn't do much. But at least we won't have to hear any more stories about ogres."

"Don't you believe it," said Zenta. "The excitement we've had here will cause rumors to spread, and in time the stories will gain in color. For years to come, mothers on the mainland will frighten their children with tales about the Island of Ogres!"

About the Author and Her Writings

Lensey Namioka has featured Konishi Zenta and Ishihara Matsuzo in seven adventure stories set in Japan during the feudal age.

She has also written a number of books that draw on her Chinese heritage. *Phantom of Tiger Mountain* is an adventure story set in thirteenth century China. *Ties That Bind, Ties That Break,* and *An Ocean Apart, A World Away* are set in China in the early part of the twentieth century.

Who's Hu? is a contemporary humorous story based on her own experiences as a Chinese-American teenager studying mathematics. Four books about the musical Yang family are set in present-day Seattle. Also set in Seattle are *April and the Dragon Lady,* a book about the inter-generational struggle in a Chinese-American family, and *Half and Half,* about a biracial family.

She has collaborated with artists in three picture books, *The Loyal Cat, The Laziest Boy in the World,* and *The Hungriest Boy in the World.* Two travel books, one on China and one on Japan, are written for adults.

Lensey Namioka's short stories and articles have appeared in many anthologies and textbooks.

The author was born in Beijing, China, and wrote her first book, *Princes with the Bamboo Sword,* when she was eight years old. Written in Chinese on scratch paper, the book was sewn together with thread.

After moving to America with her family during World War II, she studied mathematics, which she taught for a number of years before returning to her real love, writing.

She and her husband, a professor of mathematics, live in Seattle. They have two daughters and three grandchildren.